A choice too big for a broken heart

The reality of the loss of one of the most important people in his life clenched up Michael's chest and made his throat ache.

Revisiting childhood, and so much more...

"Hang on, Mom," Marlene said, leaving her memories with her footprints and catching up. "That last step is tricky."

"I guess I know how to go into my own house, Marlene. Even if I don't live here anymore."

Digging Out the Toxins of the Past

Sean had quietly wondered why his mother didn't get the house, or any kind of spousal support that anyone knew of.

Sean figured then and now he just didn't understand. Brad figured their father had weaseled out of it.

The Day All Her Best Defenses Fail

Even if she spent October in a technology and communication void, she'd know.

Some part of Sara knew exactly what day it was. Every single year.

How many last chances does one man deserve?

The last time Reggie heard Scotty's voice was the day he'd left home a few months short of high school graduation. A last grand screaming match, and his son disappeared from his house and his life.

Learning to Trust Again, Especially Herself

The next breaker rolling in on Lucy's rising guilt tide was how many huge liquor stores were probably still open, and perfectly willing to take her little brother's money.

And his fragile new sobriety right along with it.

Plurapod Pathogen

The Changes Cascade

Near Future Forward (with Jason A. Adams)

Dispatches from the Galaxy: A Space Opera Novella Trio

Dangerous Days on a Pleasure Planet

Storms of Future Past:

Dreaming the Storm

Joining the Storm

Into the Storm

Fighting the Storm

Storms of the Heart

Storms of Future Past Omnibus

Voices Through Time:

Songs in the Mountain

Secrets in the Land

Sorrows in the Earth

Walking the Ghosts

The Odd Society:

Independent by Means of Magic

Protected by Means of Magic

Collections:

Anthologies *with Jason A. Adams*:

KARI KILGORE

PASSAGES IN THE REAL WORLD

SIX STORIES OF LIFE'S TRANSITIONS

Spiral Publishing, Ltd.

Passages in the Real World:
Six Stories of Life's Transitions

For everyone who needs to remember
Change comes to us all

You're not alone

CONTENTS

THOUGHTS ON THE
PASSAGES OF LIFE

One of the clearest ways to define life is by marking change.

Our birthdays are the first and most consistent, and those serve as a milestone for parents as well. The birthdays take on significance of their own as we turn one, five, ten. Thirteen, sixteen, eighteen, twenty-one.

I'm sure I'm not the only person who wonders why there's such a lag in those celebratory birthdays once we move out of our early twenties. We slow down then, only marking the decades as they stack up.

Perhaps we don't want reminders of the years passing quite so often?

We also pay close attention to many other passages throughout a lifetime, many of them loaded with emotional significance. That baby learning to crawl, toddle, and finally walk. First words, first days of school. Losing baby teeth and sprouting new ones. Gradually taking on the physical traits of adulthood.

Some more dramatic than others.

On the far side of childhood, the milestones take on a different tone, hopefully accompanied by a sense of humor. First gray hairs, first pair of reading glasses. Admitting getting to bed early is a reward, not a punishment.

Losing all ability to tell how old someone is by looking at them. Gradually realizing people in those awkward teen and early twenties years might as well be speaking a different language.

Gaining a deep understanding of why your parents and grandparents, aunties and uncles and teachers all looked at you the way they did back then.

Having successfully reached my second half-century, I can verify a sense of humor is probably the most important thing, along with an ongoing love of learning and adventure.

You're going to need all three!

And of course there are changes that aren't easy in any sense of the word. The kind that hopefully hold off until we reach our middle years. Not that they don't cause plenty of heartache and confusion then.

Losing loved ones. Facing the reality of aging, in yourself and others. Seeing yourself and your family with a clarity that can sometimes be painful, or remarkably liberating.

Accepting how your role in other people's lives will change, hopefully for the better.

These are the kinds of stories you'll find in *Passages in the Real World*, my first collection of contemporary fiction. What you won't find are the kinds of speculative elements I so often write in fantasy and science fiction.

While we certainly can—and often do—explore the changes of a lifetime with a bit of magic or glimpses of the future thrown in, the tales in this book take place in the real world. In the here and now of modern life in the early part of the twenty-first century.

We start off with *On Choosing the Perfect Peach Dress*, which took me solidly back to my years spent in the wonderful city of Atlanta, Georgia. One of the joys of getting out and about on big holidays and special occasions was enjoying the brilliant and stylish fashion show all around us. Southern women know how to dress up with a special flair! This story ponders how to sort through all those gorgeous fancy outfits for the very best one of all.

Watching a loved one struggle with their mind

and memory creates a dreadful burden, especially when that person helped raise you. In *The Worry Trap*, I drew on memories of how lifelong challenges once easily managed can multiply over time. And how startling that realization can be for adult children still trying to figure out their own lives.

Too often when those parental changes hit, rifts between family members take center stage, whether we're ready for that or not. One of the hardest challenges can be sorting through the belongings of a house full of memories, and realizing how much you never knew. In *An Overdue Truce*, two brothers come face to face with a well-kept family secret, one with long-lasting echoes.

I approached *At the Heart of It All* meaning to write a story driven by the music computer inside my head. The only rules I set were that the songs had to come into my mind while I was writing, and that I had to either own a copy or realize I needed to get one. So the story itself surprised me as it took shape.

It ended up digging into how too many of us carry guilt or confusion about things we had no control over as kids. And hopefully how we can come out the other side with a little bit less of a burden.

In a similar example of letting the story tell me rather than me telling the story, the opening scene of *What Breaks a Man* came from a real-life experience.

While driving to Austin, Texas, several years ago for a writing conference, I got caught in horrendous traffic. I sat for what felt like an eternity in one spot, and so I naturally took in my surroundings and stepped into my imaginary would. This story surprised me with the direction it took, and left me deeply grateful it was only inside my head.

One of the surprising changes in life often hits not only parents, but friends and cousins and siblings as well. Throwing blended families into the mix can add more love, along with unexpected adjustments. Most of us have faced that bittersweet realization that someone doesn't need us as much as they once might have. And sometimes accepting that someone you love is taking responsibility for their own life. *Traditions Worth Keeping* visits a family in the midst of that shift, and the joys and fears of letting go and moving on.

I hope you enjoy these stories of life's transitions as much as I enjoyed writing them. I write to make sense of my own life and the world around me more than you might think. If you find the same kind of understanding, and possibly a little bit of comfort, that makes every step of bringing these tales out of my laptop and into the world worthwhile.

For more contemporary fiction stories where speculative elements are slight or not there at all, visit www.KariKilgore.com/ContemporaryFiction. And you'll find fiction of all kinds in almost every genre at www.KariKilgore.com.

If you want to keep up with what I'm doing next, get free stories and access to exclusive ebooks and print versions not available anywhere else, find out about Kickstarters and other fun projects, and see adorable pet photos, be sure to swing by www.ConfidentialAdventureClub.com. Hope to see you there!

And last but certainly not least, thank you for your support of me and my writing. It means the world to me and keeps me coming back to tell the next tale.

Passages in the Real World

KARI KILGORE

AUTHOR OF THE WORRY TRAP AND AT THE HEART OF IT ALL

On Choosing the Perfect Peach Dress

For all the beloved Aunties
in my life

ON CHOOSING THE
PERFECT PEACH DRESS

A untie Ellen's overstuffed walk-in closet might as well have been as big as the Atlanta Falcons football stadium downtown. Michael would have had pretty much the same chance of picking out the right dress for her last big party.

He felt like he'd stepped into the vast Easter section at Davison's, that revered Atlanta shopping institution down on Peachtree Street, circa 1983. Except everything here was better organized than any clothing store he'd ever seen. All the dresses hung at his eye level since Auntie Ellen had been a touch over six feet tall. And those dresses covered all of the available shades of the pastel spectrum, from barely there yellow to scandalously close to red.

Arranged by color, of course.

On a rack above each color grouping sat a selection of hats that came closest to matching. Any modern hat maker would be dazzled by the variety of fabrics, textures, and embellishments on display. Hardly any fake flowers or feathers here, not unless they were dyed a truly unnatural hue. There were, however, rhinestones and sparkles and strange angles and sharp edges enough to outfit the biggest church pew in the South on Retro Celebration Sunday.

Under the always appropriate below-the-knee hemlines, a pale rainbow of shoes waited within easy reach of the dresses they matched. Flats, low wedge heels, shiny patent leather. A selection of bare toe models for those extra-sassy days that called for matching nail polish.

Michael's sinuses thanked his lucky stars and the gods of allergies that Auntie Ellen never missed getting her treasured outfits cleaned just about every time she wore them. No traces of her equally Eighties collection of overly sweet perfume lingered.

Only the musty smell of the closed-off closet, neglected while his auntie had been busy dying.

Michael shook his head and sighed, wishing yet again that someone else in the family lived close enough to help him with this last duty of a doting nephew. Sure, a bunch of them would make it down to Atlanta in time for the funeral in a couple of days. They'd be there for the big shindig Auntie Ellen had mandated—no moping or mourning nonsense allowed.

He was the proudest husband on the face of the earth that his wife Trish was currently out in St. Louis, leading a seminar about the latest advances in forensic genetics at Washington University. And he was counting the minutes until she got back home for the funeral. He needed her solid understanding of his auntie's fashion sense almost as much a tight hug and her soft, reassuring voice.

But the funeral director wanted the dress this afternoon, or he was threatening to bury Auntie Ellen in that awful hospital gown that made her look even more pale and washed out than she had these last few long weeks.

Michael brushed his too-long brown hair away from his face and stared into the closet with renewed determination. *Just pick one!*

And failed yet again to make a choice.

The only thing Auntie Ellen had asked of him— besides making sure no one droned on and on about how much they'd miss her—was to be buried in her peach dress. Michael had foolishly agreed without asking any questions.

Maybe questions like what did one eighty-year-old woman need with at least thirty dresses that could easily be called peach? Or why had she insisted on keeping every single Easter frock she'd ever treated herself to going all the way back to 1959, not to mention all her little girl and baby dresses folded carefully into a drawer?

She'd even rolled up and kept her collection of cheery springtime-colored beanies and scarves and snoods that helped her through a bout with cancer back in the early Nineties, when her beautiful silver hair had fallen out before growing back in thicker and curlier than ever.

Michael was a good Southern boy, so he knew Auntie Ellen would have never committed the deep and lasting sin of being seen twice in the same fancy dress or hat on Easter Sunday.

But still, so *many*.

Maybe the most important question was how was he supposed to know which peach dress she'd meant?

He wandered over to the extra-tall white dressing table she'd had made years ago at the back of the closet, with special jewelry holders that bristled like an old-fashioned rooftop TV antenna all around the sides and back. Everything from sparkling costume pieces from her own teenage years, through her favorite big and bright Eighties plastic baubles, all the way up to simpler chains and single stones from recent years.

Once he managed to pick the dress, the jewelry part would be a lot easier. He hoped.

Michael sat heavily on a chair upholstered in (what else?) shimmering peach fabric. Or at least he thought it was peach.

Maybe that was blush? Or did it slide too far toward some particular shade of yellow he didn't know the name for?

He stared down at the black denim of his jeans, trying to clear his visual palate enough to at least narrow the dresses down to a handful. Like a light lemon sorbet between courses of an overly elaborate meal. When he looked back up, the colors blended together even worse.

This was as bad as saying or reading a word over and over again, enough times that it started to look and sound strange.

"Peach, peach," he said under his breath, not sure why he was worried about the empty house hearing his shaky voice. "Peeeeeeeach. A simple *peach* dress."

Maybe if he said it enough he'd find a way around the giant roadblock in his mind, in his heart. The one that kept reminding him that no matter which dress he chose, it would be the last one she ever wore.

He was perilously close to fifty himself, and felt stable and sane most days. He didn't exactly need his auntie to wipe his little boy tears when he escaped from stern parents, all too often confused by their overly sensitive youngest son. Or from the school and church that were determined to shove him into the correct social and career box, no matter badly his misfit edges pinched and scraped.

But the reality of the loss of one of the most important people in his life, barely twenty-four hours ago, still clenched up his chest and made his throat ache.

How his auntie would have laughed at his indecision. Not in a mean way like kids at school or his rotten cousins, but in a comforting way that somehow made Michael calm down and see how silly he was acting.

Then she'd pop up a gigantic bowl of popcorn with extra butter, and bring out an ice-cold Coke for him and a more-pink-than-peach can of Tab for herself. They'd snuggle on the flowery overstuffed sofa and watch bad movies together on the VCR while Uncle Tommy worked the night shift down at that crazy new CNN network that everyone was convinced wouldn't make it past 1990.

Michael glanced to the other side of the closet, away from the overwhelming pastel paradise. Uncle Tommy's far more sedate wardrobe hung there still, missing only the charcoal-gray suit he'd been laid to rest in.

That decision may not have been easy for Auntie Ellen nine long years ago, but it had been simple. Much like her smaller selection of at-home clothes folded and waiting in the chest-of-drawers under all those suits.

For a brief second, Michael considered pulling out the latest version of the pink sweatshirt and sweatpants she'd often worn during their all-night movie marathons, always consistent as they'd switched from VCR to cable to DVD to on-demand to streaming. Trish had helped him pick the last one out for Mother's Day only a few short months ago.

Pink was awfully close to peach, right?

But no. The color might have been unclear, but a dress was a dress. Non-dreary or not, Auntie Ellen's funeral would be in church, not in the cozy living room.

And the funeral director's deadline of three o'clock was hanging over his head with the weight of all that pale fabric.

Michael glanced at his watch to see how close the deadline was just in time to see a text message pop in from Trish.

Holding up okay, Sweetie?

He smiled and laughed to himself in the quiet closet. If anyone still drawing breath would know how much hell he was putting himself through over what seemed like a chore that should only last a couple of minutes, Trish was the one.

Still trying to pick out the perfect peach dress. At lunch?

While he waited for a reply, Michael stood and snapped a picture of the wall of Fort Pastel. He sent it to Trish, with the one-word caption *Help!*

He hoped comparing the far end of the color wheel to his wife's sensible black and darker shades of blue and green and purple would make her smile, too.

But deep down inside, he knew he'd stumble across this photo someday.

Maybe while backing up his phone, or scrolling through looking for something else. By then, the closet and the bedrooms and the living room and the kitchen and everything else would be empty of his auntie's and uncle's things. Hopefully home to a new family that would make their own lifetimes of memories where Michael had spent so many comforting hours.

A family far too young and new to understand about VCRs and real buttered popcorn and Tab.

Hopefully too close and happy to understand how much he'd needed his auntie then.

How much he missed her now.

He hoped that random photo would make him smile by then, rather than making him as sad as he was when he took it.

At faculty lunch-and-learn, Trish finally replied. *Wish I could be there, or at least call. Just pick your favorite? Your best memory with her? Love you.*

Michael sent her a series of heart emojis, then settled back down on the dressing table chair.

His best memory of his Auntie Ellen wearing peach.

That might be the only thing harder to narrow down than all those dresses.

Was it her grinning fit-to-split at his high school graduation? Dancing with Uncle Tommy at their fortieth anniversary party? Maybe wiping her tears at his own wedding, or was it all the way back to her laughing up a storm at some silly play he did in grade school?

It seemed all Michael's favorite memories of his life and his favorite memories of his auntie overlapped more than he knew.

He got up and walked over to the wall of color again, reaching out to touch the fabric. Sturdy cotton, slippery silk. Rough velvet, delicate lace.

He glanced up toward the hat parade, and his eyes went right to the collection of what she'd called her chemo caps. That was the last time he'd felt so lost and scared and alone—the night she'd told him about her diagnosis and the surgery and chemo-therapy on the horizon. He'd been dating Trish by then, but the idea of not being able to talk to his beloved auntie was too much to take.

And all at once he had it.

Michael reached up and pulled out the very first chemo cap, and the nubby texture of the hat knitted to look like dozens of perfectly peach flowers made him smile.

He'd hunted all over the city for it, back when a quick online shopping search was only a gleam in some West Coast programmer's eye. She'd cried when he gave it to her, but they were the happy kind of tears that made everyone feel better.

The first time he'd seen her wear it was Easter Sunday that same year. She'd found the sweetest dress in exactly the same color with a row of dainty lace flowers along the neckline and cuffs and the waistline of the skirt. Down at the Peachtree Street shopping mecca that had long-since changed its name to Macy's, but she always called it Davison's.

His Auntie Ellen had pulled him aside at the traditional Easter Sunday after-church feed with a wink and a grin. Just *had* to show him, she'd said. Then she tugged the cap off to reveal her nearly smooth head.

"Nothing but peach fuzz, honey. Ain't I a *sight?*"

From that day on until her hair started to grow back—and as other friends and family members joined in and her collection of chemo caps grew— she'd always giggled and told folks about her peach fuzz.

She wore the delightful caps more to keep warm and comfortable than to hide. Nothing could have suited her better.

Michael laughed and smiled at the memory, and just like that long-ago Sunday, a little crack of happy opened up in his sadness.

He gathered up that first chemo cap, along with the dress and shoes and even the fancy hat that matched. A quick trip back to his auntie's vast array of fabulous jewelry for the perfect earrings and necklace.

The last thing he needed was a small framed picture out in the living room with all the family photos. A picture of him and Auntie Ellen from that Easter, his arm around her and their heads together. She wore her peach chemo cap and the wonderful smile he wanted to remember forever.

Michael knew he never would have been able to repay her if she'd lived to be a hundred or more.

And he was proud to have his memories, and everything he needed to see her off in style.

And with love.

THE
WORRY
TRAP

KARI KILGORE

AUTHOR OF SONGS IN THE MOUNTAIN AND IN THE PINES

For everyone caught between two generations.

THE WORRY TRAP

The old home place had hardly changed in Marlene's lifetime. Her childhood home could be a vintage Polaroid photo of itself, a tiny bit faded around the edges, maybe a couple of scratches or tears, but unmistakable.

A solid one-story cinderblock foundation painted to match cheerful dandelion-yellow wooden siding above. A broad porch screened in for summer sleeping. A high peaked tin roof that shed heavy snowfalls and sounded divine during rainstorms.

A few of the merry gargoyles and critters her father had delighted in carving into the wood or setting into the foundation peeked out at her, tickled she was finally home for a visit.

Countless others waited throughout the outside

and inside, biding their time for greeting and recognition.

The grass in the tiny front yard was a bit shaggier than her parents kept it, the steep gravel driveway up the mountain more rutted with runoff than her father would have ever allowed. The same sheltering oak and maple trees showed off in their summer finery, though, and the chorus of afternoon birds sang and chirped in the woods and shallow frog pond beside the house.

The riotous flower beds Marlene and her sister Mary helped her mother tend still surrounded the yard and ran alongside the driveway. Aside from needing a few dead blossoms pruned away, the roses, daisies, and peonies were in gorgeous form.

Marlene hoped the birds had spared a few of the apples planted further up the lush hillside.

She popped a cherry cough drop into her mouth to counteract the lingering taste of acidic, overcooked coffee from the assisted living facility and grabbed her smartphone off the charger. Then she walked around to help her mother out of the minivan.

Marlene kept an eye on the placement of the older woman's green metal cane and heavy black lace up shoes on the gravel as she pushed herself out of the seat.

Gabby Everett would have shunned such clod-hoppers a few short years ago, preferring modest heels or bright lace-up tennis shoes. Same with the generic navy blue pants and plain red pullover blouse. Far too ordinary, yes, but easy to put on and wash. Gabby had never been afraid of a fancy skirt or a dry cleaner when she'd had the choice.

Those days had passed the same way Marlene's years driving sports cars had.

Far sooner than expected, way too fast to properly mourn.

Marlene followed her mother up the wide, perfectly level concrete steps her father had taken great pride in pouring himself. Marlene walked close enough to catch her mom if she stumbled, far enough back that they could both pretend that wasn't a worry.

She traced her fingers along the impressions on the inside of each step, tucked against the foundation. All the children, grandchildren, and great-grandchildren's bare feet, preserved in light gray eternity. Older generations were set the day the stairs were complete, new children added on their first visit. The larger to smaller results always reminded Marlene of Russian nesting dolls.

Her own daughter had squalled at having her

warm, soft foot pushed down into cold, wet concrete. The twenty-three years that had flown by in a heartbeat hadn't dulled the furious and betrayed look Jana flung at her formerly trusted mother, barely twenty-four herself.

Time hadn't dulled the guilt that first gnawed at Marlene that night either, holding her infant daughter on those steps in the eerie bright light of her father's Coleman lantern.

One questionable parenting decision down. Many thousands to come.

The screen door at the top squeaked the same way as always, a distinctive two-toned note that said welcome home.

"Hang on, Mom," she said, leaving her memories with her footprints and catching up. "That last step is tricky."

"I guess I know how to go into my own house, Marlene. Even if I don't live here anymore."

Marlene smiled, nodding even though her mother was already inside. This was a happy occasion, and Marlene was going to act accordingly.

Even if her mom got fussy along the way.

"How's everything look in here for your granddaughter's arrival?"

Her mother stood in the middle of the wide

porch, hands on her hips, turning from side to side. The sunlight caught her short, permed hair, glinting off the silver highlights.

Marlene hoped her own chestnut hair would be exactly the same color when she finally stopped getting it touched up.

Someday.

She'd leaned the cane against the wall, maybe expecting not to need it here. Maybe forgetting she needed it at all.

"Well, it's a dusty mess," her mother said. "Cobwebs everywhere. Looks like the floor hasn't been swept since I left. We'll have a job getting this place cleaned up for Jana."

Marlene pushed the wooden porch swing, grinning at the same gronking sound from the chains that she remembered so well. Several of her father's grinning carvings decorated the back and arms. The flowery linoleum was a bit gritty underfoot, and spiders had indeed been celebrating in every corner. But the screens looked sound and nothing was leaking.

"I think Jana will do just fine getting it cleaned up, Mom. She's so excited to be living here. I think we could tell her she had to scrub the whole place with a toothbrush and she'd sing while she did it."

Her mother grunted.

"That dust could be full of asbestos and lead and who knows what all. Better if she doesn't have to breathe it."

Marlene picked up the cane and stepped forward to unlock the door instead of responding.

Her parents had added the whole porch on, but never replaced the original entry door. The windows set into the top were still covered with one of her mother's homemade curtains. The sky-blue fabric swayed when she shoved the door open with her shoulder.

"How long has that door been sticking like that?"

"I don't know, Mom. I was last here four years ago when we got you moved. Bobby might know a little more about it."

Marlene's little brother had rented the house out a couple of times, keeping an eye on things because he still lived close by. People never stayed more than a few months, so he'd stopped bothering. Thankfully they'd never torn anything up on the way out.

"Jana could fall trying to get it open." Marlene's mother accepted the cane without hesitation. "Hurt herself and no one would know."

"I'll see if we can't get it fixed. Doesn't smell too bad in here. Just a little musty."

One of the two bulbs came on in the wavy tan

light fixture when Marlene flipped the switch. The living room stood empty except for bookcases along three walls and two lamps at least as old as Jana sitting on the hardwood floor. The cobwebs weren't nearly as thick against the light blue walls.

Her mother raised her head and sniffed. "Do you know if Bobby set off a bug bomb in here when those last people moved out? Smells like some kind of chemical."

"They moved out a couple of years ago." Marlene pulled the narrow metal blinds up and opened a window. The counterweight clanged against the frame. "I'm sure it just needs to be aired out. That could be where it's been hot in here with the air conditioner off. Bobby just got the power turned back on this week."

"Has anyone checked the basement for radon? I hear that's in a lot more houses than you'd think."

Marlene leaned against the windowsill, looking at her mother. Wondering how much could have possibly changed in the few months since she, her sister, and brother had talked to the neurologist.

Alzheimer's usually didn't move that fast, not in the beginning.

"We all grew up here without having any trouble. You and dad lived here for almost fifty years.

Jana visited most of her life, too. It's going to be okay."

Her mother pressed her lips together and shook her head. Just like Marlene had done earlier, she walked into the other room instead of responding.

"She's got furniture? Don't want her rattling around in an old empty house without a place to sit or lay her head."

Marlene snorted before she could stop herself. Hopefully her mom's hearing wasn't quite sharp enough to catch that little lapse.

Talk about making a grouchy situation worse.

"She has the stuff from her grad school apartment. Not the most expensive or highest quality, but it will see her through. Long enough to finish her dissertation, anyway."

The room was as empty as the last, but Marlene's head was full of ghosts of the high bed, tall chest of drawers, and curvy dresser with an oval mirror.

She was a clumsy kid again, trailing her oh-so-grown-up older sister Mary and trying to stay ahead of their bratty little brother, doing their best to sneak in here on weekend or holiday mornings.

Careful as they were, Marlene had always been surprised and disappointed that her parents were already awake, every single time.

"We'll have to get this water tested," her mother

said. "These old wells are full of all kinds of junk. Smells terrible."

She'd gone into the bathroom, again leaving her cane against the wall. Marlene retrieved it and turned the corner just as the older woman lifted the toilet lid. The shiny peach porcelain matched the bathtub and pedestal sink.

"I'm sure Bobby weatherproofed the plumbing. That's antifreeze you smell. The house is on town water now, Mom. One less thing to worry about."

"Well sure, you'd think so. As long as the town keeps everything running right. Don't you remember when a bunch of farm animals fell into the reservoir? Your Aunt Juanita had to boil her water for weeks before they got that mess cleaned up."

She grabbed the cane from Marlene's outstretched hand and continued on toward the kitchen.

Marlene's sister had taken on that constant worry trait when they were all a lot younger. Mary used to complain that Marlene and Bobby could have been a little more grateful to her for doing that so they didn't have to.

Marlene had learned decades ago to keep her mouth shut about seeing the same fretful behavior in her niece and nephew.

She was glad Jana was as brave as she had been,

and as brave as Bobby's kids without being quite so reckless.

For whatever reason—years passing, living two thousand miles away, or therapy she kept to herself—Mary seemed to have stopped fretting over every single thing.

She'd stopped talking to Marlene about it a long time ago, anyway.

Either something else was bothering their mother today, or her own worrying was getting worse.

Marlene caught up and touched her mother's shoulder. She peered into bright blue eyes, a mirror image of her own.

"Do you not want Jana to move in here, Mom? It's still your house, so we can talk about that."

"I never said I didn't want her to live here." Her mother jammed her hands onto her hips again, sending the cane thwacking against the doorway. "I'm proud to have her live here while she finishes her education. Your father would have been, too. There's no sense in Jana spending her money or yours renting someplace else."

"Okay, good. It's just...you seem to be worried about a lot of things you never were before. Jana's already lived on her own for five years."

Marlene followed her mother into the kitchen, wincing when she nearly fell onto a wooden bench built into the wall. The table was gone, along with the cushions, refrigerator, and range, leaving the sunflower yellow room echoing and sad.

Her mother tried to hide it, but she wiped away tears.

"You never did understand, Marlene. Things were a lot simpler when you kids were growing up. We didn't know any better. I watched out the best I could, and you all did fine. Now it would be so easy to miss something."

Marlene joined her mother, her sit bones protesting at the bare wood underneath. She stared at the white sink, focusing on the rust stain running down the middle from a leaky faucet.

Testing the water probably would be a good idea to make sure the old pipes were safe, but none of the rest made sense to her.

"Do you mean miss something wrong with the house? Bobby will help Jana with whatever she needs. You know that."

Her mother gripped the cane with both hands hard enough that her swollen knuckles turned white.

"It's not just the house, no," she said, her voice rising. "But I can't do much of anything about the rest, can I? She'll still drive too fast just like you. She'll jump on an airplane without a second thought like *all* of you. She'll still want to go skiing when the snow comes, flinging herself down the side of a mountain for no good reason. Jana doesn't think about what could happen any more than you or Bobby!"

Marlene opened her mouth, then snapped it closed. An impulsive reply caused nothing but trouble when her mother was in a good mood.

Right now her uncensored thoughts would be a disaster.

She looked up, right at a curving row of dandelions and sunflowers her father had painted on the white ceiling. A line of smiling ladybugs circled the top of the walls.

"Listen, the reason we're here is to see what all needs to be done," she said. "I'll make notes of everything, and Bobby will help Jana with any repairs. I think he's kept the place in really good shape, don't you?"

"You can repair everything under the sun in here, and everything outside too. It would still be an old house full of stuff we didn't even know could go wrong. You take all the notes you want to, Marlene. I need to take my own notes. I can't forget anything."

Marlene pulled her phone out of her pocket, knowing full well her mother wouldn't use it for any reason or reward.

"I don't have a notebook or anything. I can save whatever you want in here and print it out later."

Her mother stared at her for a second, then rolled her eyes. Despite the tense atmosphere, Marlene had to choke back a laugh at how much the gesture reminded her of Jana.

"Just as well these ugly pants have pockets since you decided I'm not allowed to carry a purse any more."

Marlene's repeated assertion—*of course she could carry a purse, as long as she let someone make sure there was no food tucked inside to rot and draw ants*—died before she could draw a breath.

She watched her mother pull out several pieces of paper, folded over and over again until they were half the size of a dollar bill, out of one pocket. A handful of blue and black ink pens came out of the other.

"I might have one of Jana's old notebooks in the car," Marlene said.

Her mother unfolded two of the papers, smoothing them against the bench.

"This will do just fine. You go right ahead and make your notes and I'll make mine. Go on."

Marlene shook her head, unable to argue with a tone she'd understood since she was a toddler. No point in arguing. Just get on with it.

She wrote down everything she'd seen so far, light bulbs, flush plumbing, test water, and got up to check the rest of the house.

Less than ten minutes later, she returned with less than twenty things to follow up on. Nothing major or unexpected in an old house, with every bit of it easy to take care of over the next week.

Jana would arrive in three days for cleaning and helping her uncle with the parts they could do.

At the end of the week, Marlene would head back to the city knowing her only child was settled in and on her last steps toward independence.

She'd share a cordial phone call with Jana's father about their little girl growing up, and she'd console herself and celebrate her daughter with good friends and a great dinner.

The problem she hadn't expected was still sitting on the bench in the kitchen, writing as fast as she could.

One page was already covered in elegant cursive handwriting that had only slipped a little with the early stages of Alzheimer's.

Marlene, Bobby, and even Mary had expected their mother to be thrilled with Jana moving in, knowing someone she loved sheltered in her beloved home. They'd talked about visits, brunches and dinners, maybe even a few overnight stays for as long as Jana was willing and had time.

When Marlene had talked to her mother about it on the phone and in person earlier today, she had seemed excited.

Right up until they parked outside.

None of them had imagined their mother getting more worried instead of less. At least Marlene hadn't.

"Want me to copy any of this?" she said. "See if Bobby or I can get started on it?"

"If it will make you feel better." Her mother didn't look up or stop writing. "Every bit of this is for me to do."

Marlene sat and picked up the page, her stomach dropping when she realized it was covered from edge to edge on both sides.

Her heart dropped when she started reading.

Asbestos, lead, radon. Test water. Bug bomb smell.

Nothing new there.

But then she saw notes to remove the propane lines because of leaks, buy electric stove. Fill in pond to get rid of mosquitos and Zika.

Make sure copperhead snakes can't get into the plumbing or walls.

Background checks on neighbors, check predator registry. Guardrail on driveway.

Emergency alert necklace since she'll be here alone.

Security system. Make sure power and phone lines can't be cut.

Water filters. Air filters. Take out wood stove so no carbon monoxide. Get monitor to make sure furnace doesn't leak it, either.

On and on and on.

"Mom, some of this...I think she'll get mad if we do all of it."

Her mother turned over the paper she was writing on and continued on the back. The scratching was ghostly and constant.

"Then don't. I don't want to forget about it."

"We've never had copperheads in the house, and hardly ever in the yard. This isn't exactly a high crime area. That's a good reason for her to live here."

Her mom stopped writing, but the pen hovered above the page, trembling with the urge to keep going. She didn't look up.

"Did I ever say this was for you to do, Marlene? Or for you to even think about? I told you this is *my* job, now leave me to it!"

Before she could start writing again, Marlene touched her wrist. Her mother's arms and hands had always been slender, but now she felt like tight skin stretched over thrumming bone.

"You don't have to remember all of this. Jana is grown up. Mary and Bobby and I are, too. You don't have to worry."

Tears dripped onto the page, the drops turning black as the ink dissolved.

"Look what you made me do! I'll have to write that part over again or I won't remember!"

She pulled her hand away and reached into her pocket for another folded up piece of paper.

Marlene knelt in front of her mother and gripped her thin shoulders. She leaned down until her mom stopped digging in her pocket and looked up.

"What's going on here?" Marlene said. "You're scaring me. Maybe we should head back and I'll finish up here later on."

"You *should* be scared!" Her mother cried openly now, not bothering to try to hide it. "Who's going to do this when I can't anymore? Not you or Bobby, and Mary has her own family to worry about."

"Do what, Mom? Jana's grown, and so are Bobby's kids. All we can do is get them ready for the world and let them go. Letting her live here is the best gift you can give her."

Her mother shook her head, squeezing her eyes closed.

"No one's watching over them, Marlene. No one

is thinking about what could happen. That's the best way to make it come true!"

Marlene sat back on her heels, rubbing her own arms against the goose bumps.

She couldn't feel more pushed out of her reasonable adult world if the floor turned to rubber and bounced her up in the air.

She didn't have to look over her shoulder to see where her mother's stove had been all her life. The last model had been a boxy harvest gold gas model that reigned for decades.

She didn't have to strain to remember her mother's repeated warnings once Marlene had finally been allowed to learn to cook. Warnings Mary happily continued if their mother was out of the room. Marlene hadn't really thought about them for years, besides relief that she could make her own rules once she finally lived on her own.

Act like the burners are always hot. You never know when they were on last.

Yes, even if no one else is home.

Make sure you know where your little brother is before you open that oven door. He could walk right into it and burn himself up. I know he's only two years younger than you.

Yes, even if you think he's outside playing.

Don't ever turn away and leave the gas on. A

breeze could blow through and light the whole house on fire.

Yes, even if there's nothing to burn and the windows are closed.

The warnings sometimes started out reasonable, but they rarely stayed that way. The same pattern applied to running bathwater, mowing the lawn, even doing laundry. They accelerated once Marlene started dating and going out with her friends.

Her mother could always come up with something that might go wrong. No matter how outlandish or unlikely, Marlene knew she'd hear it constantly.

And she was expected to act accordingly, same as Mary and Bobby. Only Mary ever really had.

Their father had done his best to keep things a little lighter and more playful, but he mostly shook his head and went back to whatever he was doing.

He often grinned and winked at Marlene and Bobby when their mother, or Mary, wasn't looking.

For the first time, Marlene wondered if that was what the carvings and drawings all over the house were for. To keep the two of them smiling instead of worrying when he wasn't there.

The scratching pen across paper again pulled Marlene back to here and now.

She settled back onto the floor, sitting with her

legs crossed like the little girl she no longer was. Her middle-aged back and hips would complain tomorrow, but it just felt right.

She touched her mother's hand again, waiting until the compulsive writing stopped.

"You know something you did when I was growing up that I made sure to do with Jana? Remember when I'd get upset and throw a fit? You'd say that was just fine. I could throw just as big a fit as I could manage. But I had to stop long enough to tell you what I was so upset about first. Remember that?"

Her mother looked up, eyes puffy and still full of tears. Her chest and shoulders rose slowly, and she breathed out hard enough to ripple the paper. A tiny smiled curved her lips.

"I remember. Worked with all three of you, but you needed it more than the others."

Marlene laughed, relieved that her mother joined in.

"Jana would probably say I still do. Can you do me a favor? I want to understand why you're so upset. Can you please explain it? Then yeah, you can write as much as you want to. We'll stop on the way out and get you a stack of notebooks."

Her mother tilted her head to one side, staring into Marlene's eyes. She finally loosened her grip on the pen and paper. She put both down on the bench and leaned back with her hands in her lap.

"Did you ever hear me or your aunt and uncles talk about Lenny?"

"Your little brother who died from polio?" Marlene said.

"That was him. I was only six when he passed away. I wanted to name Bobby after him, but my father would not have it. He said if I named that baby after the one that died, he'd never speak to me again. So we named him after your father's grandpa instead."

"Why did Papaw say that? About using Lenny's name?"

Marlene's mother sighed, and another tear escaped her eyelashes. She wiped it away.

"He said it would bring bad luck for all of us. He said we'd already had enough bad luck with Lenny getting sick because of me, and we didn't need any more."

"Because of *you*?" Marlene said. Nauseating heat surged up through her middle. "You just said you were six years old."

"I was. But Lenny was only three. Daddy said I was supposed to be watching out for him when we went out and played with all the neighbor kids. He said I didn't keep him away from the other kids like I was supposed to, and he got sick."

Marlene wished the water in the house weren't turned off. The foul taste in her mouth, stomach acid dredged up by fury at her grandfather, kept her swallowing over and over again.

"That's not fair, Mom. It wasn't your job to look out for Lenny. It was Papaw and Granny's. They were the *parents*."

Her mother flashed a lopsided smile, but it didn't reach her eyes.

"No, not back in those days. The older kids had to look out for the younger ones, not like now. We had a new little sister by then, your Aunt Juanita. I looked out for her and all the older ones, too. Juanita and two of your uncles are still alive. Your Aunt Bonnie was eighty when she died, remember?"

"I remember."

"So once I started watching out for them, none of the rest of them died." The older woman shrugged. "None of my kids did, or my grandkids or great-grandkids. You're all healthy."

Marlene covered her face with both hands, struggling for something, anything to say. Insisting to a woman in her seventies that she was imagining things she'd based most of her life on sounded cruel even inside her mind.

Add the Alzheimer's diagnosis and symptoms on top of that, and Marlene knew she'd be crossing a line she couldn't live with.

"So how did you watch out for us, Mom? Once your brothers and sisters didn't live with you, or when we moved out? What did you do?"

"I kept it all in my head. I know what might go wrong, and I never forget about it. That way I can keep an eye on those bad things and they can't get out into the world. Into your lives. That's all."

"Aren't you tired, Mom? Doesn't trying to remember all of that wear you out?"

Marlene's mother picked up the paper from the bench and refolded it. She held out her hand, and Marlene gave her the one she'd been reading so she could do the same with it.

"Not really. It's just part of my day, like breathing. The only time..."

She squeezed her eyes closed again, pulling her whole face inward for a second.

"I wasn't paying attention when your dad got into his truck that day. When that other car got into his lane and killed him. I didn't tell him to be careful on the road, to watch out for the other drivers."

"Oh Mom," Marlene whispered.

Her twisting heart told her it wouldn't do any

good to remind her mother that the other driver had been drunk and reaching for a dropped cell phone.

She knew it would somehow make everything worse.

"So now I just have to write it all down," her mother said, slipping the paper and pen back into her pockets. "I don't think I really needed to move out of this house when I did, but I have been getting more forgetful lately. I do like my new place. They take good care of me."

"They do." Marlene put her hands on the floor, getting ready to grunt and groan her way back to a standing position. "I'd like to live there with you sometimes. Do you get upset very often worrying about all of us? Like you did a few minutes ago?"

"Well no, not really. I keep all my notes in a drawer in my bedroom. The girls in the office let me have paper whenever I need it, right out of the copier or printer. Same with pens. They keep a jar on the desk just for me."

Marlene got to her feet without too much noise, mentally making notes to pick out nicer holiday gifts for the staff. She held out her hand, and her mother pulled herself up.

She left the cane on the bench.

"Once you write it down," Marlene said, "does it go out of your mind?"

"Most of the time. Some things are always there, like thinking about you kids and all the rest. But a whole lot of it stays on the paper now."

"Do you like that kind of paper? From the copier? Or do you still want to stop and buy some notebooks?"

Her mother took the cane and walked back toward the bedroom.

"Some notebooks would be good. And maybe some folders to keep the loose pages in."

"You got it, Mom. We'll pick some out on the way back."

KARI KILGORE

AUTHOR OF WICKED BONE AND THE DEFINITION OF CRIME

AN OVERDUE TRUCE

For everyone who always wondered why

AN OVERDUE TRUCE

It was the strangest thing, how houses seemed to die as soon as their owners did.

Sean leaned against the doorway to his father's home office, sort of a grandiose title for the room where the old man always paid the bills. He could still see a ghostly afterimage of his father sitting there at his plain wooden desk, most likely rescued when the old high school in town was torn down about fifty years back.

Not much more than a rectangular hulk with three drawers on each side. Almost unrecognizable compared to the sleek, angular, metal and glass structures he saw in so many modern offices.

Or had seen, before he moved from St. Louis back home to tiny Fincastle, Illinois, to help his father five months ago.

Sometimes Sean felt like enough time had been compressed into those months that people might be working from floating desks that hovered in clouds over open WiFi spots all over the world.

He snorted, then breathed in the already stale air scented with coffee and his dad's aftershave.

Walter Hopkins had been willing to trade in his high-test morning cuppa joe for decaf when his doctor insisted. But he wouldn't have given up his cinnamon and musk Old Spice for love, money, or a cure for the common cold.

The shelves his father had built along every wall and even over the windows and door were fairly simple lumber from the hardware store—the same old Ace Hardware he'd frequented throughout his life.

Never mind a TV sitcom bar. The real accomplishment for a self-sufficient Midwestern man of that generation was when everyone at the hardware store knew your name.

Sean walked slowly around the edge of the room, tennis shoes squeaking on the blue and gray linoleum, running his fingers along the white cardboard magazine holders stacked neatly on almost every shelf.

Dad had gotten a great deal on them when another store in town was closing back in the Eighties. There were probably still at least a couple hundred out in the garage awaiting their day in the sun. Or under the buzzy old fluorescent lights in the office.

Either way, the ones in the garage had run out of time when Sean's father did.

The ones he looked at now—turning in a slow circle in the middle of the room with a pit of dread in his belly—were stuffed full of decades of the records of Hopkins family life.

Precise, vertical handwriting let Sean know what was inside each. Taxes for the family and for the business that gave his father the means to pay all those years of bills. Paperwork for the mortgage, homeowner's insurance, car notes, and warranties going back to the early Seventies.

Owners manuals for every appliance and tool and at least one television from each five-year span. The Hopkins household might not have fancy cars or gadgets or the newest electronics, but they always had a fairly new TV.

An eminently practical man until he drew his last breath, Sean's father had left two of the boxes full of life insurance and other Important Papers on his humble, ordinary desk. Sean hadn't even noticed, but they must have been sitting there waiting for him since before the last mercifully short stay in hospice.

Another box labeled *Divorce* fitted in with all the others on the shelves as if it was just as ordinary and mundane as car maintenance receipts. Sean knew more about that episode from his past than he cared to, since he'd been seventeen when it happened. But the true heart of that matter remained mysterious to him.

The shifting fog and adult perceptions of his life thirty-two years later might have softened his opinion of the reasons for it all if he'd known. But his memories of the horrible months before and the slow poison of the years after were still especially vivid.

He turned to a shelf near the desk, this one entirely dedicated to medical records.

His father's, Sean's own all the way through college, and the first twenty years of his older brother Brad's life. The former Mrs. Hopkins had taken hers when she departed, and Brad never lived in this house again once the divorce was final.

He'd hardly set foot inside, truth be told. Even with the huge job ahead, Sean was relieved Brad didn't want to help with the big cleanup, either.

He loved his big brother, of course. They just didn't *like* each other very much.

The last few years took up a lot more space on the shelves as his father's illness took hold, settled in, and did its deadly work.

The house might feel empty.

Discarded. Unwanted.

Left behind after decades of careful maintenance and concern.

But there was a hell of a lot of stuff to get through before...

Whatever came next.

"Okay, young man," he said, brushing back his too-long brown hair. "All these dead trees won't clear themselves out. No matter how dead this place already feels inside."

He got out his smartphone for reference, already calling to mind the recommended length of time to keep paperwork for the state of Illinois, Social Security, the US Army for a long-ago stint, and anyone else who might have an interest.

His father had left clear and simple instructions for the rest.

Find one of those companies that shreds things and be done with it. Anything Sean or possibly Brad didn't want and no one else needed would be better off as compost anyway.

On an unusually strong impulse, the first box he grabbed was the one for *Divorce*.

He carried it over to the desk, smiling at the tiny thrill in his chest, the sensation of breaking some sort of unwritten, unspoken rule. His father hardly ever mentioned the end of his own marriage, and he'd barely commented on the end of Sean's five years ago.

He'd asked if Sean was okay, if he needed anything. Told him that was a real shame. And that was that.

Sean's mother and Brad had played up the drama a lot more, but it felt empty somehow. Contrived. Like they were determined to be more upset than he was, which wasn't all that hard to accomplish after a fairly amicable split.

Sean and Brad had fallen into their usual patterns when their mother passed away after a cruelly early case of Alzheimer's, and as their father declined physically with his mental faculties as sharp as ever.

Sean mourned gradually, noticing each change and marking each loss as it happened.

Brad pretended everything was fine until he couldn't ignore reality any longer.

Then he fell apart.

The magazine box looked kind of like an over-grown cereal box made of thicker cardboard. He pulled the top off, revealing a bottom half cut diago-nally like a ski jump. The whole thing was big enough to hold several multicolored folders: each with a labeled tab somewhere along the long edge.

The truth was he'd always quietly wondered why his mother didn't get the house, or any kind of spousal support that anyone knew of. She never actually talked about it, but Sean knew she hadn't minded if people believed his father was just too cheap. Or that she'd refused his help.

Sean figured then and now he just didn't understand.

Brad figured their father had done something to weasel out of it.

With both parents gone now and himself nearly into his fifties, the time for waiting and wondering had surely come to an end.

Before another fifteen minutes passed, Sean had his phone out again.

"Hey Brad, Sean here. ... Yeah, I'm at Dad's. I think you should come over. ... No, not to help clean up, don't worry. There's some things here you need to see."

By the time Brad finally made the hour-long drive two hours later, Sean had gotten through more of the files than he expected. One whole wall was clear—the boxes stacked up for donation, the papers in much larger boxes in the living room, ready to take to the shredding company.

He'd left a few items on their father's desk in case Brad took more of an interest. But Sean knew getting him to pay attention to closing the massive gap in their knowledge of their own family would likely be more than enough of a strain for one day.

For both of them.

The front door closed a bit more loudly than necessary, warning Sean his solitary sorting and gentle grieving time was over.

A few solid and slow footsteps down the hall, and Brad leaned his head into the room.

A little bit shorter than Sean, more solidly built, and curly light brown hair rather than Sean's wavy brunette. Otherwise no one could deny they were at least close relatives.

Same dark blue eyes, same skin that tanned more than it burned. Same body that was blocky and sort of square like their father's, face that was long and kind of narrow like their mother's.

Brad pointedly made sure his feet were still in the hallway, probably making sure Sean understood how much he did *not* want to be there.

Sean didn't need the reminder. His memories held more than enough.

"Okay Sean. I'm here. No idea why I had to drag

my ass all the way down here on a Saturday, but it was easier than arguing with you over the phone. What's this all-important thing that couldn't wait?"

Sean kept his immediate thoughts to himself. With Brad, asking if something could wait generally meant he might get around to dealing with it on the tenth of never. Which normally didn't bother Sean one bit.

But not today.

He pushed himself up from the floor where he'd been sorting through the more recent tax documents and sat in the creaky but comfortable desk chair.

"I appreciate you making the sacrifice, Brad. I'm sure Dad would have too. Listen, how much do you know about the divorce?"

Sean knew he'd messed up as soon as the words were out. Brad smirked and tilted his head to the side.

"Your divorce? Or mom and dad's?"

Brad had never quite come out and said it, but his feelings were clear. He took a certain smug superiority from being the only one in the immediate family to make it through twenty-five years of marriage. Sean wasn't sure the mutual quiet tolerance he saw between Brad and his wife Connie qualified as happy, or something he should be jealous of.

Another opinion he kept to himself.

"I mean Mom and Dad, since I'm sitting in Dad's house in front of a box labeled Divorce."

Brad shrugged, but he finally managed to walk into the room, stopping a few feet away from Sean.

"I probably know about as much as you do," Brad said. "They were unhappy for the last few years they were together. Especially Mom. It just took them a while to get around to the divorce. Probably some kind of tax scheme Dad wanted to run for the business. Kind of like he ran interference between us and Mom's family for years."

Sean sighed, sad and relieved that Brad had gotten himself to the problem so quickly and easily.

The original wedge that had split all of them in two, not just their parents.

Sean with their father, Brad with their mother.

Then and always. Maybe forever.

Or maybe not.

"Do you think it's possible there was a good reason Dad kept us from her family, Brad? That it wasn't just out of some twisted sense of spite?"

Brad snorted and crossed his arms.

"No, Sean, I don't. As far as I'm concerned, spite is all there is in this house. Did you honestly drag me all the way out here to lecture me about how I should forgive Dad? Again? He's gone now, and so is Mom. Maybe we should both just get over it."

Sean leaned forward, ignoring the chair's squawk of protest. He pulled out several pieces of paper stapled together, dry and yellowed with age, and handed them to Brad. Three were folded back and out of the way.

"I figured out a long time ago that talking to you about forgiveness was a waste of time."

Brad scowled at Sean, but the tactic worked. He looked at the papers before he convinced himself anything printed there wouldn't be true.

"What is this? Financial settlement agreement? Is this about him getting the house and her getting not a damn thing?"

Sean shrugged. "Kind of. At least the reasons underneath that. It's part of their separation agreement."

"This doesn't make sense. 'In return for previous financial assistance, Janice McShane Hopkins agrees to waive all rights to house and all spousal support.' She *agreed* to this?"

"Her signature is on the last page, same as Dad's."

"For *what* financial assistance? Mom worked her ass off to buy her place. You know as well as I do he never gave her anything."

Sean took a deep breath. Even for the chance of the clarity after decades of half-truths, he dreaded Brad's reaction if he actually took all of this in.

Looking at the reality of their family—leaving painful mythology behind—couldn't possibly be easy. Especially not right on top of ignoring their father's death and funeral only a week ago.

"He gave a lot, Brad. That's on the next page, at least the outline of it. There's another set of documents they both signed that goes into a lot more detail."

Brad's scowl deepened into a frown.

"Dad paid some kind of...what, a fee? A fine? For *Uncle Lou*? Come on, Sean, what the hell is this?"

"Just what it sounds like, really. I know you liked Uncle Lou, but a lot of us didn't. It wasn't just me. I'm sure you remember how he always gave those extravagant gifts. Gaming systems for all of us, or stereos, or whatever pair of shoes was stupidly expensive that year. All that came at a cost. And it finally caught up with him."

Brad handed the papers back. Sean was relieved he hadn't crumpled them up and thrown them in his face.

"Maybe you better let me see the other files. Are you trying to tell me Uncle Lou was stealing or something?"

"Sounds like it was white collar enough to be

considered embezzling. But stealing is close enough for our purposes. He skimmed off the top for years according to this." He gave Brad a much thicker folder simply labeled L. "Enough that Dad paid out almost half a million dollars."

Brad's face paled and he adjusted his feet, as if his knees were about to buckle. Sean got up, rolled the old office chair beside him, and leaned against the desk. He'd been relieved he was sitting when he read what Brad held in his hands right now. And even more glad he was alone.

Brad sat, slowly shaking his head, but his eyes kept moving across the page.

If what he read hit him anywhere near the way it hit Sean, Brad would be feeling more of the false fronts of their childhood come crashing down, when they'd already lived through so much demolition with their parents' divorce. Even more with the aftermath, as the four of them splintered and separated even more.

Right now, Brad probably got a brand-new gut punch every time what looked solid and stable turned out to be soft and damp and rotten.

By the time he flipped through all the crackling pages, Brad's hands were shaking. But his face was as red as his eyes when he looked up.

"How long have you known about all this, Sean?

Is this why you stayed here with him all these years? So you two could keep me in the dark?"

"You know better than that, Brad. I found out about it a good fifteen minutes before I called you. Pretty much as long as it took to read everything and decide what to do. Dad never breathed a word of any of this to me. Did Mom tell you?"

"Of course she didn't! She was too busy working herself half to death to keep a roof over her head." Even as he shouted, Brad's face and shoulders slumped from furious to sorrowful.

"I know how hard Mom worked," Sean said. "Until she couldn't any more. That half a million dollars is why Dad never retired like he planned to when we were kids. He worked up until he went to hospice, did you know that?"

Brad held the papers out toward Sean, but they floated down toward the floor before Sean could move, seesawing like dead leaves in October.

"Why didn't they tell us, Sean? We weren't babies. Why did they go through all that for Uncle Lou in the first place? That money was meant for *our* family. You and I busted our asses working too many hours all through college and got loans on top of it, and Mom and Dad worked themselves to death. And now you say he let us believe...they *both* let us believe Dad was the one who drove us all apart."

Sean shrugged, leaving the ancient separation agreement on the linoleum, a relic from an archaeological dig that might have been better off uncovered.

"I don't know. You're right, they were unhappy for a while before they split. Hell, I've always figured they should have split sooner for everyone's sake, but they did the best they could. I never heard a whisper about Uncle Lou being involved until today." He leaned over and picked up the bundle, dropping it onto the pile of unpleasant reality still waiting on the desk behind him.

"To tell you the truth," he said, "I never tried to get back in touch with that part of Mom's family after I moved out, either. I guess the last time I saw any of them was that last Christmas, remember?"

Brad shuddered, flashing a sad half-smile.

"You mean the year we all had yelling contests, to celebrate how much we were in the holiday spirit? The Shouting Christmas? Everyone in the whole house, from us kids all the way up to Gramps and Grandma. They must have all known."

"We all knew something was wrong. I doubt anyone really understood besides Dad, Mom, and Uncle Lou. That was part of the whole deal between them. Keeping it secret. Did you ever see Uncle Lou again?"

Brad scrubbed at his hair and stood, sending the chair seat spinning in place.

"Yeah. Not until I got married, and I don't think Mom ever knew. But I visited Uncle Lou a few times before he died. You probably won't be surprised he got out of the insurance business altogether. Worked as a car salesman."

Sean watched his brother walk around the room, standing on his tiptoes to peer at the highest shelves. Much like he himself did a few hours ago. As if he was looking for something they were both supposed to discover. Some kind of farewell message besides a seething mess from more than thirty years ago.

"That was part of the deal," Sean said. "The document that lays it all out has Uncle Lou's signature, too. Dad agreed not to report what he'd done as long as he paid it all back, quit his job, and left the industry. For all we know, Dad might be the one who figured out what was going on in the first place."

Brad pulled down one of the boxes that was apparently full of owner's manuals and warranties for purchases from an eight-year span in the Seventies. When he turned, Sean saw tears rolling down his cheeks.

"So Uncle Lou stole from his clients," Brad said, sitting in the chair again and rotating it to face Sean. "Or his bosses or the company or whoever. Then

Mom and Dad basically decided to steal from themselves and from each other to cover his ass for some crazy reason. But in the end, you and I paid the price without ever realizing what was going on."

Sean leaned forward, bracing his hands on his thighs. The sick, churning sensation in his gut surged up again, almost as strong as when he'd first read the words himself. Even then, he hadn't put it into words as neatly—and as horribly—as Brad just did.

"That pretty much covers it. The only thing Dad left that he wanted me to see for sure was his end-of-life stuff on his desk. As far as he knew, I was going to get rid of the rest. No way to see this in a good light, is there?"

Brad pulled the lid off, tucked it into the chair beside him, and riffled through whatever was inside. He was still crying when he looked up, but he had a ghost of a smile.

"Oh, I don't know. I hear collectors love this kind of junk. Maybe we could list it all online and cover the difference." He put the lid back on and pushed the chair into another slow spin, stopping when he circled back around to face Sean.

"If we'd found out before they were all gone," Brad said, "maybe we could have gotten some answers. Some kind of reason we could understand."

"Maybe. Or it might have gotten even more

confusing. Or more painful. You're the married man of the family now, with in-laws and all. Does any of this family stuff ever get easier?"

Brad shifted the chair back and forth, not seeming to mind the squeak every time one little bit. Sean pretended he didn't mind, either.

"I don't have anything as extreme as whatever went on between them and Uncle Lou," he said. "But I can't say it gets easier."

They lapsed into silence, but not the tense, uncomfortable kind Sean had gotten used to during their increasingly rare visits over the past few years. Visits he realized might stop completely now that they didn't have the bond of a living parent.

This was a *shared* silence. One they inhabited in a companionable way rather than as if they were trapped in a prison cell created by their mutual DNA.

Sean thought they might have last spent time together like this when they were both in high school.

Another lifetime, a long time ago.

Brad finally roused himself, getting up and taking the box full of instruction manuals back to its shelf. He crossed his arms and leaned against it.

"I'm guessing you got the house? Like I got Mom's?"

Sean raised his eyebrows and nodded.

"I guess that part balanced itself out without our participation."

"What are you going to do? Stay here, or go back to St. Louis?"

Sean smiled. "I have no idea. I can work from anywhere. I just... I haven't had time to think about it yet, you know?"

"Yeah, I know. I ended up selling Mom's, but it was a beast to clean out and get ready."

He ran his fingertips along the boxes, then looked back at Sean.

"I'm really sorry, Sean. About everything."

Tears prickled at the back of Sean's throat. He'd called his brother out of...anger or resentment or maybe a weird sense of obligation, with no idea what he was trying to accomplish or what to expect.

Maybe simply so he wouldn't have to know about this bizarre arrangement alone.

The last thing he would have imagined if he'd taken the time to imagine anything was apologies.

Long-overdue, but sincere, apologies.

"I'm sorry too, Brad. I think we've been fighting a battle neither one of us started. One nobody understands any more."

Brad started to cross the room toward Sean, but stopped, leaving Sean in an awkward half-standing hunch.

"Listen, I can't stay too long," Brad said, now not meeting Sean's eyes. "Got a lot going on at home. I drove the truck, though, so maybe I can help you sort out some of this for a little while. Then help haul off a couple of loads if you're ready. To the dump or to get them shredded or whatever you want."

No, it wasn't a typical sappy, over-the-top Hollywood reunion. Maybe not even one fit for a moody arthouse drama. Thirty years worth of problems between them couldn't be solved in a couple of hours after one nasty revelation.

But it was a start.

The two of them working together might even breathe a little bit of much-needed life into the house they'd both grown up in.

"That would be great, Brad. Grab your medical records, and I'll get the rest of this tax stuff. Maybe we'll hit the jackpot with all those owner's manuals after all."

KARI KILGORE

AUTHOR OF IN THE PINES AND THE WORRY TRAP

AT THE HEART
OF IT ALL

For those of us with Earworm Brains

who understand how music can save lives.

AT THE HEART OF IT ALL

E arly evening was Sara's favorite time of day. Winter or summer. Home or work, or on vacation. No matter where she was or what she was doing, an elemental and vital part of her relaxed when the hour hand pointed straight down.

This six in the evening found Sara in her vast, nearly empty office building, almost at the end of her workday. The door to her small office open as usual, music playing through her computer's speakers as always. She could walk across the whole tiny room in five quick steps, but the pale wooden desktop had no need to accommodate anyone's coffee cups or elbows but her own.

Cream-colored walls held her own artwork, the shelves her own silly toys and mementos. No calendar, not this month, but one featuring classic electric and acoustic guitars would return in a few days.

The option to turn off the harsh overhead light in favor of a sweet lamp shaped like a tree branch–complete with a cardinal perched in the leaves–was one of the best parts of having her own space at work.

But not nearly as important as having the music.

The small cubicles and shared desks out on the main floor offered no such escape from glaring light overhead and cramped workspaces with barely enough room for a monitor and a mouse. A few other late-workers from the day shift in the huge medical records center lingered, huddled over transcriptions or translations. The low murmur of one-sided phone conversations so prevalent during the day had vanished, leaving only sporadic office chit-chat.

The night shift on the data entry side wouldn't arrive until eight or later, leaving Sara and a handful of others to enjoy the lull.

The one thing she did envy about the main floor that she didn't have in her office was a wall made of windows. Right now, the setting October sun transformed the bland walls and empty tan cubes into a red and orange and purple wonderland, glittering with islands of coffee mugs and monitors at just the right angle to return the light.

A scene Sara's father would have wanted to

paint, to transform into one of the visions he saw in his head. *Visions in Blue* by Ultravox flitted through her mind, but only for a second. From 1983, the same year she was born.

Sara caught herself still staring into the strangely enchanted space when a low chime interrupted her computer playing Beck's *The New Pollution*. Her mind filled in the details as she turned back to her right-side monitor. From *Odelay*, his second proper album, released in 1997. She'd been waiting on that batch of new patient records to import so she could verify the integrity of the data, but that was no excuse to sit and let her mind wander.

She shook herself, clicked through the notifications of record mismatches, and focused on the left monitor while the import continued. Thousands of new records wouldn't be much good to anyone if Sara didn't finish designing the tables for them.

Beck giving way to Gordon Lightfoot made her smile at the little surprises of her own music playing on random. *If You Could Read My Mind*, album of the same name.

"Hey Sara? Got a minute?"

She turned to see Jake, her supervisor for the last few months. Her belly flushed warm at his grin and his gorgeous eyes. Elton John's *Blue Eyes* fanned the flames in Sara's middle until she was afraid her chest and neck were turning red with the heat.

She hit pause on the Gordon Lightfoot, afraid that would only make her skin's overreaction even worse.

"Sure, Jake. What's up?"

He leaned against the open door, crossing his arms.

"I was trying to think of a song, but I can't remember enough of it for Google. My sister wants only music from the year I was born for my fortieth birthday." He rolled his eyes, but now he was blushing. Sara thought it was just about the sweetest thing she'd ever seen. "Smile while you can, Ms. Don't Bother Making a Fuss about Me Turning Thirty-five. Anyway, the song. A lot of saxophone and guitar, and something about a street, maybe?"

"*Baker Street*," Sara said with no hesitation. "That's Gerry Rafferty."

At Jake's raised eyebrows, she knew her cheeks were blazing. She should have pretended to think about it, at least. She usually knew better.

"Wow. You really do have a music computer in your head. That's amazing."

His smile seemed real, though, and he wasn't trying to back away.

"Yeah, it comes in handy from time to time."

"I hope you can make it to the party. Let Sis know if she makes a mistake?"

Men at Work sang out a warning in Sara's mind before she answered too quickly. *It's a Mistake.*

"I won't say a word if I notice, at least not to her. But I'd love to come."

He nodded, grinning again.

"About got that new batch of data sorted? Have to make sure the weekend crew has something to keep them busy."

Sara chewed her lip, determined not to quote Loverboy of all things to her boss who she had a huge crush on. Even if *Working for the Weekend* seemed too perfect to ignore.

"Just cleared them to process through. They'll be ready before they get here at eight."

"Great, thank you. Night."

Sara waited until he was out of sight, and hearing range, before she closed her eyes and sighed. It was about time for her to pack up and head home herself, especially if she was going to act like a goofy school-girl. *Stupid Girl* by Garbage popped up in her mind to try to make her feel bad, shoving her too close the dangerous ground of the early 90s. She only shook her head.

She couldn't afford to react to such a weak opening attack, and certainly not so early in the day.

Worse would be along before this day turned into tomorrow.

Much worse.

Not wanting to risk even the quick walk out to her car without protection, Sara had her earbuds in and her mind on modern things before she closed her office door. Lady Gaga and *Poker Face* established the current century again, and reminded her of a lofty goal to work for with Jake.

Just play it cool, is all. If she could manage to not act like a dork, they could keep building up a friendship. Sara hadn't had many friends over the years. So even if it never turned into more, it would be worth it.

She gave in to her mind's slightly dirty demands once she was in her sedan with the doors closed, queuing up Roxy Music's *More Than This* on her phone and through the speakers. Sara liked their 70s music better most of the time, but *For Your Pleasure* would likely set off Jake-centered daydreams too distracting for rush hour.

Sara's father had gotten her into all this music from before she was born. He'd pretty much installed the music computer in her mind that Jake and so many other people had been impressed by. Everywhere she'd ever worked, the word somehow got around and people asked her about songs constantly, but Sara didn't mind. She liked the safe reminders of her dad.

She may have been born with the computer, really, but her father had at least installed the software and optimized it for music. The massive database she'd been filling as long as she could remember. Anything that changed after that hadn't been his fault.

She shook her head, muttering under her breath.

"Not now. Not while you're in this traffic."

She took advantage of a dead stop on the highway and called up Jimi Hendrix and *Crosstown Traffic* to distract herself.

Keeping the calendars out of her office helped some with this dreadful, painful month. Same with turning off the displays on her phone and her computers at work. Even if she'd followed her occasional impulse and spent all of October in some sort of technology and communication void, she'd know.

Some part of Sara knew exactly what day it was.

Every single year.

Smashing Pumpkins took over in her mind, insisting *Today* was what she needed to hear no matter what her phone was playing. No matter what she didn't want to be reminded of. Sara changed to the radio, deciding this was an ideal time for her regular expeditions into new music. Nothing like concentrating on learning new songs and lyrics to keep things under control.

That was one of the things that made her mother's suggestion of getting into computers, into IT, so appealing when Sarah was finishing up high school and at loose ends of what to do with her life. Always something more to learn. Safe ways to direct her concentration. Different tasks and technology to lose herself in.

New ways to try to direct and quiet her mind. Constant changes.

The clatter and jangle of commercials only opened new cracks in the layers of shields in her mind, so Sara switched away from radio. Bowie's *Changes* replaced the noise, slipping her into a less frantic mental gear just as she accelerated out of the slow crawl of commuters and onto her exit.

She missed the days when she could volunteer for overtime to keep herself out of trouble. When she'd worked grunt level jobs with managers and co-workers who were always desperate to find someone to fill in, overnight if she was lucky. One problem with getting promoted was people depended on her for certain hours of the day. Her skills were too specific now to change her hours around so drastically.

And Jake would notice if she volunteered for a

data entry shift. He'd be concerned about work flow for her vital database administration work, sure. But he and Sara had gotten close enough that he'd ask questions she had no desire to answer.

She pushed the gearshift into Park in front of her cookie cutter white house with black shutters, grabbing for her earbuds before the music cut off. Keeping something playing at all times was her best defense today, the only way she'd found to minimize the pain.

Silence gave that music database in her mind too much freedom to torment her at will.

George Michael's *Freedom* 90 was uncomfortably close to the year Sara would spend the next several hours struggling to avoid. But it would work to keep her occupied on the walk from the curb to the sidewalk to the boring white front door.

The oddly shaped isolated cul-de-sac gave her privacy, but it kept her from the distraction of neighborhood greetings or gossip on a night like this. When she could really use the small talk for a change. Her mind played along for a while, reminding her that the year was only in the song title because Wham! had a song with the same name only five years before.

A much happier time in Sara's life for certain,

1985. Not many memories lingered from her third year, but they were all good ones.

Watching her father practicing his guitar and singing, learning song after song. Her mother home as much as she could be from her early law practice. Both of them delighted and laughing and applauding when Sara started mimicking her father, singing along as best she could.

Her own high-pitched voice and little girl lisp belting out *Take Me Home, Country Roads* burst out of her memories, drowning out the music in her ears as easily as she'd drowned out John Denver and her father on that night still so crystal-clear in her head.

She had to try three times to get the key into the lock with shaking hands, adding more scratches to an already scarred brass surface. She dashed inside and slammed the door, leaning against it and trying to catch her breath.

Not quite eight o'clock, and already it started.

Sneaking through, slipping past, spilling over. Even with the earbuds, having its way with her before the night really got started.

Sara felt a cold, hard certainty that singing as loud as she could wouldn't help her this year.

Most of the time it did. She'd bought this relatively isolated house so she could do just that. Turn the music up as loud as it would go and sing herself hoarse, often until the sun rose on the morning of October 25th and she had a whole year to recover.

That's what she'd expected to do tonight since tomorrow was Saturday. Get through the dreadful anniversary and move on. But if pumping songs almost directly into her brain with earbuds wasn't going to help tonight, neither would a sonic assault from speakers and a stereo that cost more than her car.

She tried anyway, connecting her phone and holding her breath until Chicago and *Saturday in the Park* filled her living room. She'd never heard her father playing this one, only singing along if it played on the radio. Not enough guitar to catch his true interest.

Of course anything past 1991 should be fine. Safer. Less likely to trigger the cruel side of her mind, lingering underground all year long but fighting its way through to surface and control her every October.

Elvis in her mind broke through Chicago in her ears then, offering up *Don't Be Cruel*. Sara laughed, but it was a desperate, choking sound.

1956. The same year her father was born.

She covered her eyes, not bothering to cover her ears. She'd never worked out how to cover the ones inside, so why worry about that?

"Look around," she whispered. "Find something here to focus on. At least for a little while."

Dire Straits whispered through her mind in return, echoing *Why Worry*.

Sara dropped her hands, taking in her neat and orderly and sadly bland living room. She'd barely focused on anything besides the stereo since she moved in five years ago. Shiny wooden floor, robin's egg blue walls, navy blue curtains. Unremarkable brown fabric sofa and loveseat and chairs. Cheap coffee table and end tables.

Then the only thing that truly mattered to her in the whole house. The wall of shelves that held her expensive stereo and everything that fed both it and the monster in Sara's mind.

A blinking light on one of the end tables drew her eyes back and sent her heart surging into her throat. Maybe someone had called from work, maybe *Jake* had called. Offering long, drawn-out apologies followed by a blessed request for her to come back in after all.

An emergency.

An escape.

A chance to recover before she sank too far down into the pit inside her head.

Sara staggered toward the house phone, stabbing her finger at the playback button before Nine Inch

Nails and *Down In It* could get too comfortable in her skull.

"Hey hon, it's Mom. I know you like to keep to yourself today, but I'm worried about you. You're the same age he was now. That year. When...when he..." A soft sigh. "Just give me a call if you need to, no matter what time. Love you."

Sara took in a deep breath and held it.

That was it.

That was why.

She'd refused to celebrate her thirty-fifth birthday back in July without really thinking about it. Just another year passing, right? Why get excited about that one? It wasn't even a big deal, not like thirty or forty or fifty. She understood Jake letting his sister make a big deal about his fortieth, but she'd resisted even an office cake for herself this year.

Because her father had been thirty-five. He had *turned* thirty-five.

The night he killed himself.

She let out her breath and gulped in another one, stopping the music streaming from her phone as she sank onto the loveseat. Maybe her internal jukebox wouldn't be quite so vicious if she stopped resisting. Another slow, deep breath brought The Police with it, and *Every Breath You Take*.

The three of them had gone out to dinner for his

birthday that night, and her father seemed fine. Cheerful and happy, more so than he'd been for a long time. Even at eight years old, Sara had noticed the difference.

He'd been so sad and down. Barely speaking, never smiling.

And her mother so anxious and worried about him hadn't exactly eased Sara's mind.

That night Sara had gone to bed relaxed and fallen right asleep.

Everything was going to be okay. All of them were going to be safe now.

Until her mother woke her with a scream that still echoed in Sara's ears when she didn't force it away or drown it out with music.

That question echoed, too. The one she still asked sometimes when she drifted off to sleep, even the soft songs she played all night long not quite keeping it at bay.

Why?

What had happened?

What had they done?

What had *she* done?

The Eagles drifted through her thoughts, singing the same thing Sara's mother told her over and over again. That night and the next, and the next week, and the next month and year.

I Can't Tell You Why.

Her mother said she didn't *know* why, over and over again. He hadn't told her anything or left a note. No clue, no hint what really happened. What drove him to leave them behind in such a horrible way.

Back then, when Sara was eight and ten and thirteen, and she never stopped asking, she decided her mother was just keeping it from her. Trying to protect her from some mysterious adult thing she wasn't old enough to understand yet. So she waited.

She only asked once a year. On October 24th. And she got the same answer.

She stopped asking when she turned eighteen, not bringing it up again until she turned twenty-one. And twenty-five. And thirty.

That was another thing she'd refused to do this year, on her birthday or since. She hadn't even asked the question. Not to her mother, not to herself.

She wasn't sure if she'd given up or simply accepted. All she knew now was that she didn't want to ask anymore.

One more deep breath, in and out, a breath that finally relaxed her exhausted body and reeling mind.

Sara started her music streaming again, waiting for The Moody Blues to bring their own *Question* into her living room. Her father had learned this one to exact guitar and singing perfection, with the same passionate study he'd brought to every song he learned.

The same passion Sara continued to this day with her own never-ending pursuit and intake of music.

She played her mother's message again, letting her tears fall at how hard the voice on the recording was trying not to cry.

It had been her mother who taught her. Told her what to do. On one of the endless, agonizing nights when the two of them tried and failed to make sense out of the whole thing.

One too young to understand. The other too lost in her own shock and grief to pretend she understood. Too honest in her bones to make something up to comfort her sobbing daughter.

"Listen to music with him," she said, holding Sara close and rocking her to sleep. "On the stereo when you're here. In your mind when you're not. In your heart. That's where he lives now, for both of us. That's where it all lived for him, too. All that music. In his heart."

Sara wiped her tears, safe and calm within her mind for the first time since she'd left work. Maybe for the first time in years, since everything fell apart.

Maybe she could finally stop falling apart inside herself.

She tapped out a text message to her mother before bringing up one more song.

Tough night, but I'm okay. Give me a call if you want to talk. I finally found the perfect spot for one of Dad's guitars, too. Bring one over and spend the night if you're up for it.

We'll both feel better tomorrow. Love you.

Sara kicked off her shoes and curled up on the loveseat, smiling and closing her eyes as one of her father's most practiced and beloved Rush songs wrapped her up in a great, warm hug.

The closest she'd felt to her father–and to herself–since twenty-seven years ago on this same night.

Closer to the Heart.

KARI KILGORE

AUTHOR OF THE WORRY TRAP AND AT THE HEART OF IT ALL

WHAT BREAKS
A MAN

*For everyone who struggles between
holding on too long and letting go too soon*

WHAT BREAKS A MAN

Reggie gripped the bottom of the hot, sticky steering wheel, focusing on the ache in his scarred and swollen knuckles. The snarled construction traffic inched forward just often enough that he couldn't put the car into park and stretch his cramped right foot. The oily stink of exhaust floated through the open windows to compete with the reek of weed and cigarettes ground into the stained, faded cloth seats. Motionless, humid air did nothing to clear out the sweetish aroma of gas from the hatchback.

Now that he was stuck in it, Reggie felt guilty about making his kid drive this heap even after the air conditioner quit working.

The decaying, grubby black padding was missing

along the top of the steering wheel, and the dark exposed metal was too hot to touch after baking in the July Texas sun for days. Reggie had yelled when his son picked the rotten foam off when he was sixteen, wondering why he was so stupid even with a fifteen-year-old beater of a car.

Scotty had answered with a shrug, as usual, before slamming his bedroom door. That surly kid hadn't stopped trying to escape his screwed-up family since the day he was born. Not much different than Reggie, really.

Except Scotty may have finally managed the trick this time.

Reggie leaned forward and pulled his wet t-shirt away from his back even though it was useless with the sweat-soaked seat. The oil-stained work cooler in the filthy passenger floorboard only had a couple of cheap beers floating in more water than ice. He could still taste the bitter remains of the last one in the back of his throat, and the flavor wouldn't be any better lukewarm.

That didn't mean he wasn't going to pop one of the disgusting things open to wash down a couple of Percocets before this blasted traffic broke up.

The eighteen-wheeler on his left ground its gears loud enough that Reggie flinched away, then it jounced forward before the air brakes hissed. The interstate ran though a concrete gully of half-built overpasses, perpetually delayed by some corrupt politician or other, concentrating the fumes and dust into a toxic haze.

Even with dozens of Texas license plates between pulsing brake lights caging him in, no one was taking the exit just ahead. The steep ramp looked abandoned somehow, with weeds growing in the cracks in the pavement and drifts of garbage along both sides. Stubby, broken pillars of concrete fringed with twisted exposed metal rebar jutted out from the walls above the highway, all that remained of a strangely absent bridge.

Voices whispered up out of Reggie's brain, crawling down his neck and twisting his already tight shoulders. Take your work GPS, his buddies down at the garage said. The boss won't know. Don't want to get lost down there in the ass-end of nowhere Texas. Just throw it in your suitcase. Don't be an idiot.

If you're going on this fool trip, they said, at least ditch your damn stubborn pride and get a smart phone.

Ignoring the latest dig about dropping a fortune on a pocket computer when he didn't even own a flip phone was easy enough. So was leaving the chattery electronic travel brain safely at home, tossed in the floorboard of Reggie's latest dealership employee special. Much as it got on his nerves when it demanded he take a u-turn or recalculated for what felt like hours, the thing would have given him a way out of this snarled traffic.

Maybe even that exit, the one no one had ventured onto while cars and trucks inched and braked, inched and braked.

The idea of his expensive work-trip nanny sitting on this cracked and faded dashboard felt obscene, anyway. The gadget was probably worth more than the whole car.

The only link to the outside world was one Reggie hadn't paid or planned for. A small grey pager, so ancient he thought it might have been a derelict from the 90s, tucked in the glove box along with a drift of old registrations and solidified ketchup packets. The thing fit in his palm. Nothing but a tiny one line screen on the end, a built-in belt clip, and a couple of shredded rubber buttons, like someone was in the habit of digging at them with a key.

It powered on, but he had no idea whether it was activated or what the phone number could be. Everything that might have identified it had been scratched off, maybe by that same key. Reggie had slipped it into his pocket, still not sure why.

Another voice, one Reggie was more likely to scream at than listen to even after thirty years, whispered through his mind. Why are you driving this rolling death trap, then? Drop it off at the closest junkyard and let the crusher do its work. Better yet, park the nasty thing right here and walk away. They'll either tow it away or let it rot and crumble in the sun.

Then his own voice.

You know how to walk away, Reggie.

Instead of letting that settle into the space between his ears, Reggie jerked the steering wheel to his right, getting a shuddering response from the leaky power steering pump for his trouble. His right foot ached to stomp on the gas pedal, if nothing else to get a fresh breeze through the windows. Dealing with a stalled engine on top of everything else might force him to discover what he did when a day like this finally broke him, so he eased forward instead.

The gap he'd left in the endless line of vehicles closed before he got all four wheels onto the ramp, a gleaming orange Hummer jumping ahead in a heartbeat.

Decision made, then. Get on with it.

For what had to be the hundredth time in the seven or eight miles he'd managed of a thousand-mile trip, he wished the heap had a manual transmission. The creaky old automatic whined higher and higher on the sharp grade of the off-ramp, but it refused to change gears.

Maybe with a stick, Reggie could downshift, hit the gas, and launch this whole disaster over the other side of the ramp. Crashing on top of some perfectly maintained suburban SUV—breaching the fine-tuned climate control and yanking the overly pampered driver out of cell phone oblivion—would be worth a couple of scrapes and bruises.

Reggie shook his head and craned his grubby, aching neck, trying to get the lay of whatever land he'd just rolled himself into at a blazing fourteen miles an hour.

The desolation and decay of the highway didn't improve with the change in elevation. A row of low concrete barricades, shoved out of line and piled up with garbage, made a halfhearted attempt to stop cars from driving out into nothing. Reggie wondered how long ago the highway department forgot this place ever existed.

That temptation surged in him again, the desire to see how many of the blocks he could ram over the edge before the junker died.

Or before someone stopped him.

The ramp he'd expected, and halfway planned to follow back onto the highway, was blocked by more of the same crumbling barricades. Unless he was willing to take his chances and reverse back down into the nightmare traffic jam, turning right was the only option. The road was nothing but old concrete slabs, faded to nearly white and full of cracks. It cut straight through a vast industrial wasteland full of rusting shell buildings and empty parking lots before curving off to the right.

No other vehicles up here, though, clogging up the freeway and the air. Even better, no people.

Reggie didn't have much choice, but he still felt a tiny thrill of satisfaction when he turned and kept going.

He realized his mistake after less than five minutes of following slow curves through acres of wasted factories and dead grass.

Without the crush of cars and people to keep him angry and distracted, his thoughts kept veering back to the same sickening topic like the car trying to drag itself to the left.

The dealership's chirpy receptionist over the echoing garage intercom, telling everyone within earshot that there was a call for Reggie Cox. Straightening from the boss's late Sixties Camaro, wiping his hands to keep from smudging up the office phone.

That voice on the other end, clear enough to hear how hard Scotty had been breathing, even though the kid was whispering.

Trouble.

Some kind of trouble, big enough that Scotty would be disappearing for a while. Probably a long while.

Reggie too shocked with a phone call after years of silence to insist on knowing, understanding, before the kid hung up.

Maybe asking if he could help.

He slowed the junker, the one he'd made his son drive to supposedly force him to learn to work on them like the old man. Grabbed one of the warm beers. Swallowed half of it with the Percocet.

Before that day had ended, Reggie had somehow booked a one-way flight to Texas. He didn't remember making the call, but the charge to his credit card showed up along with the ticket in his work email the next day.

Stupid, that. Not having a computer or smart phone meant he only used email that didn't even pretend to be private.

A smart phone might have shown him the number Scotty called from, too.

He did remember cracking into more than beer once he got home. He'd found the empty bottle of Wild Turkey in the trash the next morning, staggering around the kitchen wondering what smashed his head with a baseball bat overnight. That explained the plane ticket.

His least favorite voice piped up in his head, as usual when Reggie'd done something even though he should have known better.

You didn't have to get on that plane, son. You could have reported that credit card stolen, shut the whole thing off. Or just eaten the cost and not made this whole mess worse by throwing yourself into the middle of it.

"Thanks, Mom," he said, not surprised by the rough edge to his voice. "Always knew how to make it all worse in the end."

Reggie forced his attention back to the road, hitting the brakes hard enough that the heap skidded sideways. A row of modern black and yellow barricades stretched across, blocking what looked like another several miles of abandoned industrial wasteland.

Why the hell hadn't someone done that on both sides, or blocked the highway exit?

A well-maintained road cut across his path, fresh black pavement and bright white lines as far as he could see in both directions. Still no houses or any other kind of buildings, but this had to be better than driving deeper into nothing at all. His tour of dead American manufacturing jobs wouldn't get him any closer to Ohio before he had to be back at work or lose his own job.

He considered for a second, looking at the sinking sun to find west, tapping his chewed fingernails on his leg. He'd probably hit some kind of civilization faster if he turned right again, toward the medium sized city he'd come from. Where Scotty had been living. But he'd be going south, making a longer drive for himself in the end.

The nearly full gas tank, typical for an old car you checked the oil in before the gas, made his choice for him. North it was.

Reggie's mood even brightened for a minute. A cool breeze blew his hair back as the car finally topped forty miles an hour, and the Percocet was starting to kick in. If only he had a stack of old cassette tapes on the seat beside him, he could be the guy in his early twenties on a road trip.

His whole life ahead of him, as vast and endless as the arteries and veins of asphalt across the continent.

But Scotty was the one in his twenties, not creeping up on fifty like Reggie. And just like Reggie, he'd closed off one of those paths after another, barricades made of anger and rock-solid grudges instead of concrete putting him on the same predictable path.

Scotty hadn't knocked up his high school girl-friend and given up on college, then never let that girlfriend forget it. But he had run off before he even finished high school, then gotten himself caught up in something terrible down here. Something so bad he hadn't even thrown it in Reggie's face to point out what a failure he'd been as a father.

Reggie jumped so hard he jerked the steering wheel when the pager buzzed against his leg. Only the sluggish power steering kept him from driving straight into the concrete drainage ditch that was his only companion through dusty farmland all around. He fumbled the thing out, hoping he could manage to activate the ancient screen.

Digging his fingertip into one of the shredded buttons rewarded him with a phone number he didn't recognize followed by 911. Old pager talk for *call right now* unless things had changed. Call right now, with no cell phone and the odds of finding a pay phone slim to none no matter where he was. The area code was strange too, like one of the new ones for an overcrowded city, or only for cell phones.

None of that mattered unless he could find a phone, any phone. Reggie put the pager carefully on the passenger seat, afraid of draining what had to be a primitive battery. He nudged the car up to fifty-five, close enough to the last speed limit sign he'd seen.

His mind, his own voice instead of his mother's, protested that getting pulled over for speeding would be a perfect way to end this trip early. Depending on what Scotty had done, police might be looking for even this junk pile. Or that pager. They'd certainly be wondering who'd broken into Scotty's apartment, using the same credit card to defeat the cheap lock.

The place had been surprisingly neat, nothing like the room Scotty had tried his best to destroy at home. It barely looked lived in. Beige walls, tan furniture that would fit in at a doctor's office. The sign out front said apartments, but Reggie would have sworn he was in one of the extended-stay hotels the dealership put him up in when he had to travel for training.

Going on nothing but some kind of vague notion that he was helping Scotty, he'd gathered up the few things he was sure didn't belong there. The garbage bags in the kitchen and bathroom. The hatchback stank so strongly of gas that it covered up the faint rotting food smells of the garbage. A couple of shirts and socks that looked like they'd been dropped. A few books. Anything he thought someone could follow back to his son.

The key he'd had already, stashed away years ago in case Scotty locked himself out. He never had, at least not out of the car.

The road finally curved toward the left, back

toward the highway, and Reggie spotted clusters of houses on both sides in the distance. When he got closer, several more sprouted up against the farmland. He barked harsh laughter when the tall blue and white sign of a gas station towered over everything else.

He got the heap parked in the lumpy parking lot, dug several quarters out of his pocket, and grabbed the pager. Maybe, just maybe this place was run down and faded enough to still have a pay phone lurking inside. The wrinkly cigarette ads covering the smudged windows had to be a good sign. If nothing else, maybe he could bribe the kid behind the counter to use the phone back there.

He found neither in the fog of stale smoke and overcooked coffee, but the scrawny girl agreed to let Reggie use her cell phone for the low fee of five dollars. Reggie wondered how much she'd pocketed with that little trick, but he handed the money over and walked to the other side of the store. The rows of glass-fronted beverage cases had seen better days, and they'd surely been cleaner. Reggie wanted any privacy he could get.

Someone picked up on the first ring.

Scotty.

"Who the hell is this?"

"It's your father, Scotty. What's going on?"

"You have my car or just the pager?"

Reggie took a deep breath, blowing out condensation on the glass.

"I have the car. I thought it would be better if no one could find it."

"I don't think the car's going to make much of a difference at this point."

"Scotty, what's happening? What can I do?"

"Are you on a cell phone?"

"Yeah," Reggie said. "Not mine, though."

"I didn't think it would be yours. But someone might trace it. I won't be here for long, so it won't—"

"Tell me where you are, or at least a phone number! Let me do something to help you."

"That's what I was trying to do. Got a pen or something?"

Reggie walked back up front and grabbed a pen and a piece of receipt from the register while the girl fiddled with the fountain soda machine.

"I'll be at this number in an hour," Scotty said. "How did you know where I live?"

"You're still on your mother's insurance, remember? She gave me the address. I didn't tell her why. You called me for some reason, son. Tell me what's going on."

Scotty sighed.

"I shouldn't have done that. We'd both be better

off if you just went back home. Go buy a cheap cell phone, one without a contract. Call me in an hour. No promises."

A click, and he was gone.

Reggie stared up at the fluorescent lights overhead, one buzzing, one out. A scattering of dead bugs dotted the plastic covers. He blinked away tears before the girl could see them, thanked her, and left.

He sat in the car, face in his hands, trying not to shiver in the lingering heat. His damp shirt and the clammy fabric seat didn't help. Neither did the images tearing through his mind.

The last time he'd heard Scotty's voice was the day he'd left home a few months short of high school graduation. A last grand screaming match, and his son disappeared from his house and his life.

Scotty's mother left not long after. Reggie couldn't think of a single reason for her to stay, no matter how long and hard he tried.

They both knew they'd only been staggering along in their marriage for years, hoping they could somehow make their son turn out okay.

Reggie had shown her part of what he'd found in Scotty's room when he pulled down a bunch of ratty old posters and a couple of framed photos.

The kid had punched holes in the drywall,

evenly spaced and methodical. Like he was trying to beat the house until it gave up and fell down.

Reggie had never shown or even told anyone about the rest.

On the back of those posters, Scotty had scrawled on every inch of space. Some of it narrow and cramped, some sprawled and looping.

Horrible filthy language and even worse ideas. About everything and everyone in his life.

Especially his parents.

Reggie had read as much of it as he could decipher, unable to stop, knowing he'd remember the words and the fury and the imagined deeds for the rest of his own life. He'd crumpled the posters up and sat on his son's bed, sick and shaking, until his wife got home.

Exactly like he was sitting in the car Scotty had driven off in years ago.

A few miles down the road, he found a cell phone store and bought the only non-smart phone they had. No contract, free activation, a thousand minutes. The clerk told him about a cheap motel a little further on.

Reggie had time to check in, shower with harsh soap and scratchy towels, and call Scotty at exactly the promised time.

He had to look at the room phone to tell his son where he was.

"That town is a pit. Why the hell did you stop there?"

"So I could talk to you, Scotty."

The pause went on until Reggie was sure the call had dropped or he'd managed to turn the phone off.

"You're better off not knowing," Scotty finally said. "Go home. Tell yourself I'm somewhere doing just fine."

"I don't care about any of that. You're my son."

"Okay, you had your chance. I killed five people last week. Didn't plan to. Might have been a set up, to tell you the truth. But it's done."

Reggie closed his eyes, wondering if it was too late to stop now. Scotty's voice was calm and cold. He could have been talking about buying groceries or taking out the garbage.

"Bunch of guys I work with." Scotty barked laughter too much like Reggie's. "Used to work with. Doing odd jobs no one else wants, cleaning up messes not near as bad as the one I'm in. They all stayed in a duplex on the edge of town, run down dump of a place. Anyway, had trouble with all of them at one time or another. You know how it is."

Reggie did know. Scotty had had *trouble* with almost everyone in his life from the time he was in grade school. His bedroom walls weren't the only thing he'd tried to beat to death.

"So I heard from our boss, the one we did the odd jobs for. Said these guys told him I was stealing from him. Taking money off the top of what I collected, keeping things I'd picked up for myself. Whatever else I am, I ain't a damn thief. I asked a couple of them and of course they denied it. But they never did have a good word to say about me."

Scotty paused, then blew out his breath loud enough to make the phone rumble. Reggie saw his son in his mind then, just as he'd been when he left but bigger. More filled out.

Sitting back in his chair, legs crossed with his ankle on his knee. Brown hair spiked up, half-smoked cigarette in one hand no matter how much his parents begged and threatened. Reggie smelled the menthol and tobacco smoke so strongly he fought back a cough.

"They were all supposed to be on a job out of town," Scotty said. "Boss told me that's why he had me doing grunt work that day, because they were all gone. Well, like an idiot I believed him. I drove over there that night, splashed gas on the siding and dead bushes, and lit the place up. I was too angry to think straight, I guess. Didn't check to see if they were actually home."

"But they were."

"Sound asleep. No smoke detectors in the place, or maybe they were too drunk to hear them. I didn't even know until the next day. That's when I panicked and called you. Arson in Texas is bad enough. Once you throw murder on top of it, you're talking a first degree felony. That's the rest of my life in prison, but they might love the death penalty down here enough to try that, see if it sticks. Got to head south and stay there."

"The gas in the car," Reggie said, his voice weak.

"What?"

"That's why I smelled gas. I thought it was a fuel leak. In the car."

"I didn't even notice that. Taking the heap up to Ohio might really help me out, then. You should take it on to a junk yard where it belongs. Or push it into the river."

Reggie nodded, aware Scotty couldn't see him, but with no idea what he was agreeing with. His heart pounded in his ears, his body ran hot and cold. His brain so sluggish he might as well be drugged.

His son.

This was his *son*.

No matter how things had turned out, this was the laughing little baby who'd held on to his pinkie finger so tight it hurt. The smiling toddler who giggled madly as he ran off every chance he got. The little boy who loved nothing more than cuddling up between his parents when they were watching TV.

That boy had grown into a man, and that man was a murderer. The only thing Scotty seemed to feel bad about was that he might get caught if he didn't run far enough.

"Yeah, probably should junk it," Reggie said. "Not much else to do. Junk it and everything else."

He squeezed his temples with his fingers and thumb, trying to make sense of anything inside his skull.

Could he walk away and pretend this never happened? Force himself to forget what he knew, never tell another person as long as he lived? Let Scotty run off to Mexico and hope to never hear from him again?

Hope that was far enough that he never heard of anything else Scotty did, no matter how bad?

The hell was Reggie didn't know if that would be easier to live with than turning Scotty in. Sending his only child to prison.

"That sure would help me out," Scotty said. "Biggest mess I've got myself into since the old woman's statues or dolls or whatever she called them."

Reggie's heart stopped, then lurched painfully in his chest.

"The old woman? You mean your grandmother?"

"Yeah, don't you remember that? Thought Mom was going to hold me down so Grandma could kill me." He cackled again. "Death by old lady."

Reggie remembered. More than he could stand to deal with while Scotty was on the phone. He held his breath for a few seconds, then forced himself to start talking.

"You need money, son? I can get my hands on a little bit. A few thousand."

"Course I need money. I didn't exactly have time to plan ahead for this great escape."

"Listen, I know you don't have a lot of time. Are you close enough to get here tonight? I can leave it in the glove box. I'd rather see you, maybe take you out for a decent meal, but in case you can't stop."

"I...yeah. I can get there. By sunrise for sure. I'd hate to wake you up, long drive tomorrow and all."

Reggie swallowed hard, checking himself over inside and out. Trying to decide if he could go through with this.

"I understand, son. I have to run out and find an ATM, but that shouldn't even take an hour. I'll get out as much as I can. Remember the name of the place?"

"Well great! Yeah, I remember. You really came

through for me, Dad. I'll try to make it in time to say goodbye."

This time, Reggie ended the call himself. The hard calm surging through his mind and body scared him, but he knew he'd use it as long as it lasted.

He gathered up all his things, then drove the heap about five minutes to a bank he'd spotted on the way in. He drew out a few hundred dollars in twenties, enough to look good in a bundle. And enough to bribe the motel clerk to check him out early, call a taxi to the airport, and keep his mouth shut.

Reggie left the money and the pager in the glove box and dropped the key in a drain grate on the other side of the parking lot.

He waited out the ride to the airport, the same one he'd flown into. Ten minutes with no traffic.

Out on the curb, he used the cheap phone to call the police. Anonymous tip, easiest thing in the world.

Yes, he thought the arson suspect would be at the hotel sometime in the next few hours.

No, he didn't have anything else to say.

The phone's battery went into a garbage can. The phone went into the bottom of his suitcase, soon to end its days at the bottom of a river in Ohio.

The last flight out was in a couple of hours, but Reggie thought that would work out just fine.

He didn't know if anything else ever would.

All he knew was he was thankful all the damn voices in his head kept their opinions to themselves for a change.

First thing when he got home, he'd go visit his mother-in-law. Former, technically, but Reggie never felt like he divorced her. He never wanted to. She'd been a thousand times the mother to him than his own managed, even when her memory started to go.

Her most prized possession in all her homes and in her room at the assisted living was her collection of figurines. Silly little things. Pastel painted girls and boys, cats and dogs. A couple dozen or so, carefully collected throughout her life. She always wanted them lined up where she could see them first thing when she woke up.

A few years ago, those figurines had turned up broken when she was out at a doctor's appointment. Not only knocked off, but smashed. Ground into the rug with someone's heel from the looks of it.

Reggie's wife had insisted she'd handle it with the staff herself.

Reggie had insisted on sitting with his mother-in-law that night and again the next day. Her soft, child-like crying wrecked him, breaking his heart more than the day his own mother died. He held her hands as she whispered *why* over and over again.

Scotty ran off less than a week later.

Reggie paced around his nearly empty departure gate, orbiting his suitcase.

The kid had a decent chance still. If he got there sooner than the cops, he might get away.

Get away with it.

Again.

Or he might not.

That was up to him and up to fate.

Reggie vowed to do everything in his power to never find out.

KARI KILGORE

AUTHOR OF THE WORRY TRAP AND AT THE HEART OF IT ALL

TRADITIONS
WORTH
KEEPING

For everyone who understands
we all need recovery

CHAPTER 1

What should have been an unusual Thanksgiving seemed oddly traditional, almost normal, until Lucy spotted the strange thing in the refrigerator.

The formal dining room of the house she'd grown up in positively glowed with harvest feast cheer. The sturdy oak table that had almost always been round while she was a kid sported all three leaves, transforming it from a table for four into a long table for twelve.

A broad rusty-orange runner down the middle was new but welcome. With the heavy fabric embellished with acorns and autumn oak leaves and bundles of crimson cranberries, it made the old table feel brand new.

A line of stout golden candles marched down the

middle of the runner with little wreaths of leaves around the bottoms. None of them were lit yet, but Lucy thought the candlelight would be lovely against the rippled glass in the big china cabinets.

Those cabinets—passed down through her father's family for generations—mostly stood empty today. Twelve places were set with tan plates accented with a raised green vine all around the edges, another new touch Lucy quite enjoyed. The first kids' table they'd needed for many years had a similar festive air adjusted for the under-eighteen crowd.

Turned out her mother had been happy to leave the massive cabinets behind, but she wasn't about to leave her own mother's white china with gold edging. The cabinets remained here in St. Louis, while Lucy's mother, her china, and not all that many other things had made the trip up to Chicago about eight years ago.

Out in the living room, an overwhelming number of people gathered around the brick fireplace Lucy remembered and loved so. Not watching football, not yet. That would wait until after what promised to be a belt-and-pants-loosening dinner.

Instead the crowd was actually talking (a modern holiday miracle), with phones only in use to show off photos of vacations, pets, and family members who weren't there for their first blended Thanksgiving. Sharing the tart and delicious cranberry spritzers that her father's new wife Tina had made after Lucy suggested leaving alcohol off the menu.

Tina, who'd married Lucy's father back in the spring, had done amazingly well at the hard task of fitting into Lucy's tight-knit family, as well as into her childhood home. Today's test of the first major holiday together was a tough one that showed promise of going well.

Lucy only hoped the day continued to go well when her brother Jacob finally arrived.

Tina and her oldest son Greg had brought out cute trays of sliced fruit, vegetables, and cheese. Enough to keep everyone happily getting to know each other without getting hangry, but light enough that the main event would still be appreciated. A plate of tiny little slices of pumpernickel bread harkened back to Lucy's Seventies and Eighties childhood, while the whole-grain crackers kept everything grounded in the present.

Tina had confided to Lucy that she'd bought it all pre-sliced to save time and cut down on stress, a big party approach Lucy heartily approved of.

Lucy's wife Jana was currently settled in with their new nieces and nephews, showing off photos of the dogs and cats they'd boarded back in Atlanta.

The idea of having four-legged cousins had tickled the kids from the first time they'd met, and the demand to see pictures always followed close behind the greeting hugs.

Lucy had spent the last hour happily engaged with their herd of new step-brothers, exchanging childhood exploits they were willing to talk about in front of their parents. Lucy understood perfectly that even well into your thirties and forties, some of the questionable activities of youth were better left unsaid.

Still, she'd jumped at the chance to come out to the kitchen when the supply of spicy brown mustard for the bread ran low. Not out of a desperate need for teeny little sandwiches, though that had her internal nostalgia gauge pleasantly in the red.

Lucy wanted a moment to herself. A brief bit of time to think, to settle down the strangeness of having people who'd only been in her life for a couple of years gathered in her lifelong home. And trying her best not to mention Jacob in any of her youthful exploits that involved alcohol left her in a swirling undercurrent of sadness and regret.

Worry about what might happen when he showed up didn't mix well with memories of how badly things had gone for him at dad and Tina's wedding.

She ignored all the various side dishes either in progress or fully prepared all over the cooktop and the huge granite island in the kitchen. Her mouth watered and her stomach growled at the amazing scent of the silvery foil-covered turkey resting on the counter. Tina and Greg had given the one-hour warning a while back when they brought out more spritzer and took their chance to join in the gossip and chatter for a bit.

Lucy and Jana were much more of the we'll-go-out-for-a-big-meal-with-friends variety than cook-at-home types, but Lucy admired the planning and coordination happily on display.

Instead of checking on things—and interfering with Tina and Greg's arrangements and careful timetable for the meal—Lucy went straight for the big double-door stainless steel refrigerator. A much-needed upgrade of a crotchety old Nineties model Tina had been perfectly right to refuse to put up with.

And that was when she spotted the strange thing, at least to her Midwestern-turned-Southerner eyes. The fridge was packed full for the day, of course, and she'd have a challenge picking a small jar of spicy brown mustard out of the other jars and boxes and bundles and cartons.

There, right on the second shelf down on the left,

sat a jar of Duke's Mayonnaise right beside a jar of Kraft Miracle Whip.

Lucy stared for a second, then snorted out laughter.

No, this would never make any sort of news or society commentary, in the South or the Midwest. Tina's North Carolina origins, making her technically another Southerner, explained the odd import. Pretty much anyone outside of those regions probably wouldn't understand what had struck Lucy so funny.

If she hadn't been so over-peopled already this afternoon, she might not have either.

But whatever the cause, the essential tomato sandwich condiment of the South sitting so comfortably alongside the Midwestern staple made Lucy giggle. It somehow represented the oddity of finding herself in a newly blended family when she was forty-four years old.

She sighed and shook her head, then snaked her hand along the crowded top shelf and grabbed the mustard. The only person who shared her odd combination of smart-ass and sentimental humor was Jacob, and he was a good half an hour late going by his last text saying his plane had landed.

She fought back a wave of guilt about not finding a way to pick him up at the airport instead of listening to his calm insistence that he'd get himself to the house. She and Jana had flown and taken the train instead of renting a car, but asking her dad to borrow his wouldn't have been unreasonable.

The next breaker rolling in on the rising guilt tide was how many huge liquor stores were between the airport and their father's house. All of them probably still open this early on Thanksgiving, and perfectly willing to take her little brother's money.

And his fragile new sobriety right along with it.

"Get a grip, Lucy," she said quietly. "He keeps telling you, Jana keeps telling you, your therapist keeps telling you, mom and dad keep telling you." She took a deep breath and told it to herself. "I am not my brother's keeper."

She almost dropped the mustard at a deep voice from right behind her.

"Never thought I hear you say *that* out loud."

Jacob stood there, backpack in hand, grinning like the goofy, exasperating kid he'd been before so many things went wrong. His wavy brown hair was a little shaggy around the edges, but the neat beard suited him.

Best of all, his face was no longer swollen and puffy and blotched with broken blood vessels. And his blue eyes were clear and alert.

Jacob looked healthy and happy.

Lucy hugged him tight, relieved she didn't smell anything more than the brisk cold outside on his brown coat or his breath, upset with herself for checking.

He hugged her back harder than he had in a long time.

"I was about to call out the search party," she said.

"I know, I'm really sorry about that. Getting out of the airport was insane, and Rick and I got to talking. Entirely my fault. I should have called you."

"Well, I'm glad you're here now," Lucy said. "Everyone will be. Is Rick someone we knew from high school?"

Jacob managed to tuck his coat into the overstuffed coat rack by the kitchen door, then dropped his backpack under the multicolored clutter.

"Nah, he's my sober-buddy up here. We've been in touch for a few weeks, ever since I decided to make the trip. He offered to pick me up, get me to a couple of meetings, drop me off on Saturday. I wanted to walk in on my own today, but he'll say hi at some point. He's a good guy, Lu."

Lucy blinked, surprised and then embarrassed. She'd tried to keep her voice calm and her face neutral instead of suspicious, but probably hadn't managed. Either that or Jacob knew what she'd been thinking earlier about him stopping by every liquor store all the way here.

She hadn't exactly been quiet or overly trusting in the past.

"Sounds like he's a great guy," she said, smiling and hoping her face wasn't too red. "And you *look* great, Jacob."

He ducked his head and blushed, reminding her even more of the sweet kid he'd been so long ago. The general din of conversation got louder, then started moving toward them.

Apparently they'd decided the turkey had rested long enough.

"You look great too," Jacob said. "Married life suits you. Sounds like I made it just in time. I'm *starving*."

CHAPTER 2

Lucy forgot all about the scandalous Miracle Whip/Duke's arrangement as she watched Jacob greeting everyone back in the dining room. A smiling Greg got the first hug on his way back into the kitchen, his tall, lanky build and short blond hair quite a contrast to Jacob.

Greg's easy and enthusiastic welcome set the tone, and the whole crowd followed suit. Lucy spotted her dad wiping at his eyes around the same time Jana caught her doing the same.

"How's he doing?" Jana said, slipping her fingers through Lucy's.

"He seems good to me. Has a few meetings planned, and someone to talk to up here. Calmer than last time."

Lucy couldn't bring herself to mention the

wedding, not while she was looking at everyone so relaxed and happy. That day, she'd tried to get Jacob to talk to her, to explain why he was so tense and keyed up. Why his face looked too thin and too puffy at the same time.

He'd been sober for a year by then, but he didn't seem the least bit stable.

She'd finally understood when she walked around the corner in the reception hall, barefoot and quiet because her shoes pinched horribly.

She'd caught Jacob slipping a black flask back into his tuxedo pocket.

An entirely predictable and whispered fight followed, one Lucy felt bad about every day since. Turned out Jacob hadn't taken one sip out of that flask when she caught him.

He'd just drained it. And not for the first time that day.

By the time he stormed off, no longer whispering, the big dose of booze had kicked in. After a few choice and very loud words to the whole family that Lucy still didn't want to think about, he'd left. Thankfully in a ride share rather than driving himself.

He'd checked back into rehab a couple of days later.

And Lucy had started her own therapy.

Today, she didn't see a trace of that furious Jacob. The one that still lurked inside her mind, ready to pounce and lash out in her nightmares.

Jana squeezed her hand and brought her back to the much more pleasant reality.

"How are *you* doing, sweetie?"

"I'm good, too. Calmer than last time myself."

"Well, I'm thankful for that. And I'm thankful that Tina and Greg are about to stuff us all silly."

By the time everyone got settled around the long table—with the gorgeous turkey and ham and every side dish known to humanity making Lucy's stomach rumble and stretch in anticipation—she was surprised to see Greg reach up to the only occupied shelf in the china cabinets. He passed around a set of delicate and lovely champagne flutes she'd never seen before.

Unlike her mother's intricate cut crystal version, these were plain except for a line of tiny flowers etched around the rim and spilling down to the stem on one side.

New vessels for an old tradition Lucy hadn't expected to see this year: saying what they were thankful for and toasting past and continued good fortune.

With champagne Jacob did *not* need even a sip of.

Lucy shot a worried look at Tina, but she only smiled and nodded toward Jacob seated to Lucy's right.

"Don't worry," he whispered. "I've got way too much to be thankful for to make everyone skip this part. Greg's got me covered."

Greg walked back out of the kitchen just then, with a bottle of pale champagne in one hand and a pitcher of the pink cranberry spritzer in the other. About half the adults and all the kids with their plastic glasses joined Jacob in skipping the alcohol.

He grinned and mouthed *It's okay* when Lucy hesitated in her own choice.

She filled her own glass and Jana's with the champagne.

And she found her eyes welling up even more than usual with what everyone had to say.

Starting with the kids and their sweet words about days off school and their new Grandpa and even their new furry cousins, to the adults with more somber but still heartwarming new jobs, good health, and being part of a new family.

Lucy was most thankful they hadn't skipped this part after all. Especially when Jacob held up his glass full of fizzy pink.

"I'm thankful to be *here*. Right here, with all of you."

Lucy took the time to look each person in the eye while blinking back the tears in her own.

"I'm thankful for all of these new beginnings."

CHAPTER 3

W andering around the kitchen of her family home at just after midnight certainly wasn't a new tradition.

Going back to sometime in her early teenaged years, Lucy had enjoyed the chance for peace and quiet after a day full of way too many people.

That and the opportunity to pick at the leftovers unobserved brought her awake and heading downstairs every time whether she wanted to or not, as if years of experience set an internal alarm clock she couldn't adjust.

The kitchen reflected the big crowd even after a marathon group cleanup after dinner. The sleek black dishwasher's glowing green light meant it had finished its third run of the day. Yet the warm golden glow of the nightlight beside the gleaming double-bowl sink reflected off of a packed-full dish drainer.

All the household's impressive supply of sturdy knives, wooden spoons, and cutting boards sat tucked in with actual silver silverware, a delicate gravy boat, and crystal champagne flutes. Managing to share the space and fit together despite their different functions and rare acquaintance.

Much like their newly blended family had during the day.

The black granite of the center island was almost totally hidden by covered plates full of football-and-conversation snacks along with desserts that had survived the massive feast.

The St. Louis staple of unnaturally red and exactly-too-spicy-enough Red Hot Riplets potato chips sat beside the folded paper box full of the crunchy Southern goodness of cheese straws. The first another vital ingredient of Lucy's childhood spent in this house, the latter imported by Lucy and Jana from Atlanta.

Decadent St. Louis-style gooey butter cake shared space with a proper fruity Southern hummingbird cake full of pineapple, pecans, and cream cheese frosting, both nearly demolished.

The whole Thanksgiving feast had reflected the same mix of traditions old and new, Midwestern and

Southern, familiar and foreign to various members of their new family.

The scent of turkey, ham, and fresh-baked bread still lingered in the air, and Lucy was amazed her overstuffed belly had room to manage any kind of protest.

She was finally old enough to recognize she'd be better off supplying its demands with ginger ale or tonic water rather than more food.

The soft whisper/thud of stocking feet on the hardwood floor warned her she was about to have company on her tonic water run. Maybe even Jana, braving the house she insisted was frigid cold in search of hot chocolate, or maybe a simple glass of warm milk.

Jacob popped his curly brown-haired head around the edge the kitchen door instead.

"Should have known you'd be down here raiding the wreckage," he said. "Any turkey left?"

None of the furtive glancing around Lucy remembered, or annoyance that someone else was up.

Only an open, honest smile that warmed her heart.

"I haven't touched the turkey or anything else. It's all yours." She opened the fridge door and waved him over. "Check this out, though. See anything strange? I might just have been living in the South too long."

He laughed under his breath.

"Okay, that is weird," he said, reaching in for the plate full of turkey all sliced and ready for leftovers. "I don't think I've ever seen mayo in the fridge here at all, much less that brand. Mayo is usually Hellman's around these parts, if it's there at all."

"*Exactly*. I think Tina brought it, along with the Cheerwine." Lucy retrieved the little bottle of tonic water she greatly preferred to Cheerwine's cherry cola flavor and settled onto one of the barstools around the island. "Well, I'm not being fair. Tina brought a lot more than that. Dad seems really happy."

Jacob nodded as he moved around the fridge and the kitchen, retrieving thick whole-wheat bread, lettuce, and dill pickles. Lucy couldn't help smiling at his choice of ordinary yellow mustard in a barrel-shaped container rather than mayo or Miracle Whip. He found an empty space on the island barely large enough to hold it all, then got a small plate out of the dishwasher.

"He does," Jacob said. "That's wonderful to see. I think it took him longer to get over the divorce than it did Mom. Once she knew it was time to go, she'd already done the hard part, you know?"

Lucy and Jacob had visited their mother in Chicago many times, but she made it clear she was finished with big stressful holiday gatherings.

"Tina is good for Dad," Lucy said. "This whole day has been great."

Jacob put together most of his turkey sandwich with the ease and speed of years of leftover raids.

"Definitely," he said. "Kinda strange, though, don't you think?"

Lucy pointed at his sandwich, which he was currently topping with a handful of the bright red and super hot potato chips.

"You're doing *that* and asking me if something is strange?"

"Oh come on. You're the one who taught me how when we were kids. On more than one hangover morning if I remember correctly, or late-night fits of the munchies when you'd been into something else."

He put the second slice of bread on top, picked the whole thing up, and took a big crunchy bite, staring at Lucy the whole time.

At the memory of the spicy hit of the chips, her jaws ached and her mouth actually started to water.

Right on schedule, her guilt showed up. Over the role she might have played in his later struggles, when he drank so much that he never stayed sober long enough for hangovers to surface.

She took a long drink of the bitter, refreshing tonic to wash it all away.

"Yeah, yeah, I remember. I can't imagine eating that way in the middle of the night anymore. Okay, what do you think is strange?"

Jacob crunched and chewed, humming contently to himself, and chased it all with a drink of the unnaturally red Cheerwine.

"*This* stuff is strange," he said, "but good. No, I was talking about new people being here. Not so much Tina, but her kids. We've known them for a while, sure, but we haven't been big-holiday close. Hell, just eating in our dining room with someone else's plates and napkins and stuff had me a little off-balance."

"Might want to hold on to your barstool, then. Have you realized Tina's kids are our *step-brothers* now? All four of them?"

Jacob stopped with his sandwich halfway to his mouth and stared at Lucy again, his eyes so wide she covered her mouth to keep from laughing too loud.

"I honestly hadn't even thought about that," he said. "So we're two of *six* kids?"

"You got it. Even better, I'm not the oldest, and you're not the youngest. Not anymore."

Jacob repeated his sandwich and Cheerwine routine, shaking his head.

"I hadn't really planned on acquiring four new siblings in my forties. How are we supposed to handle steps, anyway? Who forgot to give us the instructions?"

Lucy shrugged. "I'm not sure if it's a bigger change for you to have a bunch of brothers instead of one sister, or for me to be the only girl in a whole herd of stinky boys."

"I just got three more sisters-in-law, too." Another bite, another drink, and a wink at Lucy. "No wonder I'm in recovery."

She tried to fight it, but the laughter bubbled up anyway.

There was the smart-ass brother she'd been missing.

For the first time since she'd realized how much trouble he was in so many years ago, she felt comfortable talking to him about it. Actually *talking*, not scolding or yelling, begging or pleading.

"You seem different to me, Jacob. Relaxed somehow. More settled, maybe."

"Well, better than the last big family gathering for sure. I'll take that as progress."

"What do you think changed?"

He put down the crusty remnants of his sandwich and brushed red crumbs from his beard.

"I let myself get too freaked out about the

wedding. The whole idea of dad getting married, the family changing again." He shook his head once. "No, I'm sorry. That's not right. I didn't pick up the booze again because of a wedding. I picked the booze back up *first*. So of course I got right back into the whole confused mess in my head and everything turned sour and bad. If I don't want that to happen again, I can't take the first drink. That's all."

Lucy took a deep breath, wishing she could get everything sour and bad out of Jacob's head and out of his life forever.

And knowing she couldn't, no matter how much she wanted to.

"That's a lot. I'll do anything I can to help, you know that."

Jacob tilted his head to one side, then the other.

"I know you would, Lu. But listen, no matter what I might have said when I wasn't thinking clearly, it was *never* your fault I got into trouble with drinking. Nothing you did or didn't do caused it. Nothing with mom or dad, either. So yeah, I'm glad you're all on my side, every single day. And when it comes down to it, I have to get through this on my own. Every single day. Every hour. Sometimes every minute. But it's getting better. Okay?"

Lucy closed her eyes, letting his words and the

relief that came with them find their way into the anxious grooves and wedges inside her mind.

Where she'd taken on more of his trouble than she'd realized, at least before she started digging into her own struggles and quirks, and thoughts that too often felt sour and bad.

Where she too was getting better.

Every single day.

"Okay." She reached out and gripped his shoulder for a quick second. "Same here, brother. Same here."

Jacob finished up his Cheerwine and smiled. "So I'll see you and Jana at Mom's for Christmas? Got my sober buddy and meetings lined up and everything."

"You will. Quite a bit different with only the four of us after today."

"Yeah, we won't have to fight over dessert. Sure you don't want anything to eat?"

Lucy considered for a second, watching Jacob slide a bit of the hummingbird cake and the gooey butter cake onto his plate. She got another plate and two glasses out of the dishwasher, then grabbed the milk out of the fridge.

"Load me up," Lucy said, pouring for both of them. "Some traditions are worth a bit of indigestion in the morning."